Love's Match

A Lilac Lake Book

by

Judith Keim

NOVELS BY JUDITH KEIM

THE HARTWELL WOMEN SERIES:

The Talking Tree – 1

Sweet Talk – 2

Straight Talk – 3

Baby Talk – 4

The Hartwell Women – Boxed Set

THE BEACH HOUSE HOTEL SERIES:

Breakfast at The Beach House Hotel – 1

Lunch at The Beach House Hotel – 2

Dinner at The Beach House Hotel – 3

Christmas at The Beach House Hotel – 4

Margaritas at The Beach House Hotel – 5

Dessert at The Beach House Hotel – 6

Coffee at The Beach House Hotel – 7

High Tea at The Beach House Hotel – 8

Nightcaps at The Beach House Hotel – 9

Bubbles at The Beach House Hotel – 10

Canapes at The Beach House Hotel – 11 (2025)

Sea Breezes at The Beach House Hotel – 12 (2026)

THE FAT FRIDAYS GROUP:

Fat Fridays – 1

Sassy Saturdays – 2

Secret Sundays – 3

THE SALTY KEY INN SERIES:
Finding Me – 1
Finding My Way – 2
Finding Love – 3
Finding Family – 4
The Salty Key Inn Series – Boxed Set

SEASHELL COTTAGE BOOKS:
A Christmas Star
Change of Heart
A Summer of Surprises
A Road Trip to Remember
The Beach Babes

THE CHANDLER HILL INN SERIES:
Going Home – 1
Coming Home – 2
Home at Last – 3
The Chandler Hill Inn Series – Boxed Set

THE DESERT SAGE INN SERIES:
The Desert Flowers – Rose – 1
The Desert Flowers – Lily – 2
The Desert Flowers – Willow – 3
The Desert Flowers – Mistletoe & Holly – 4
The Desert Sage Inn Series – Boxed Set

SOUL SISTERS AT CEDAR MOUNTAIN LODGE:

Christmas Sisters – Anthology

Christmas Kisses

Christmas Castles

Christmas Stories – Soul Sisters Anthology

Christmas Joy

The Christmas Joy Boxed Set

THE SANDERLING COVE INN SERIES:

Waves of Hope – 1

Sandy Wishes – 2

Salty Kisses – 3

THE LILAC LAKE INN SERIES

Love by Design – 1

Love Between the Lines – 2

Love Under the Stars – 3

LILAC LAKE BOOKS

Love's Cure

Love's Home Run

Love's Bloom – (2025)

Love's Harvest – (2025)

Love's Match – (2026)

OTHER BOOKS:

The ABCs of Living With a Dachshund

Trouble At The Winston Hotel... A Mouse Mystery

Holiday Hopes

The Winning Tickets

For more information: **www.judithkeim.com**

PRAISE FOR JUDITH KEIM'S NOVELS

THE BEACH HOUSE HOTEL SERIES – BOOKS 1 – 10:

"Love the characters in this series. This series was my first introduction to Judith Keim. She is now one of my favorites. Looking forward to reading more of her books."

BREAKFAST AT THE BEACH HOUSE HOTEL – *"An easy, delightful read that offers romance, family relationships, and strong women learning to be stronger. Real life situations filter through the pages. Enjoy!"*

LUNCH AT THE BEACH HOUSE HOTEL – *"This series is such a joy to read. You feel you are actually living with them. Can't wait to read the latest one."*

DINNER AT THE BEACH HOUSE HOTEL – *"A Terrific Read! As usual, Judith Keim did it again. Enjoyed immensely. Continue writing such pleasantly reading books for all of us readers."*

CHRISTMAS AT THE BEACH HOUSE HOTEL – *"Not Just Another Christmas Novel. This is book number four in the series and my introduction to Judith Keim's writing. I wasn't disappointed. The characters are dimensional and engaging. The plot is well crafted and advances at a pleasing pace.*

MARGARITAS AT THE BEACH HOUSE HOTEL – *"Overall, Margaritas at the Beach House Hotel is another wonderful addition to the series. Judith Keim takes the reader on a journey told through the voices of these amazing characters we have all come to love through the years!*

DESSERT AT THE BEACH HOUSE HOTEL – "It is a heartwarming and beautiful women's fiction as only Judith Keim can do with her wonderful characters, amazing location. and family and friends whose daily lives circle around Ann and Rhonda and The Beach House Hotel.*

COFFEE AT THE BEACH HOUSE HOTEL – "Great story and characters! A hard to put down book. Lots of things happening, including a kidnapping of a young boy. The beach house hotel is a wonderful hotel run by two women who are best friends. Highly recommend this book.*

HIGH TEA AT THE BEACH HOUSE HOTEL – "What a lovely story! The Beach House Hotel series is a always a great read. Each book in the series brings a new aspect to the saga of Ann and Rhonda."*

THE HARTWELL WOMEN SERIES – Books 1 – 4:

"This was an EXCELLENT series. When I discovered Judith Keim, I read all of her books back to back. I thoroughly enjoyed the women Keim has written about. They are believable and you want to just jump into their lives and be their friends! I can't wait for any upcoming books!"

"I fell into Judith Keim's Hartwell Women series and have read & enjoyed all of her books in every series. Each centers around a strong & interesting woman character and their family interaction. Good reads that leave you wanting more."

THE FAT FRIDAYS GROUP – Books 1 – 3:

"Excellent story line for each character, and an insightful representation of situations which deal with some of the contemporary issues women are faced with today."

THE SALTY KEY INN SERIES – Books 1 – 4:

FINDING ME – *"The characters are endearing with the same struggles we all encounter. The setting makes me feel like I am a guest at The Salty Key Inn...relaxed, happy & light-hearted! The men are yummy and the women strong. You can't get better than that! Happy Reading!"*

FINDING MY WAY- *"Loved the family dynamics as well as uncertain emotions of dating and falling in love. Appreciated the morals and strength of parenting throughout. Just couldn't put this book down."*

FINDING LOVE – *"Judith Keim always puts substance into her books. This book was no different, I learned about PTSD, accepting oneself, there are always going to be problems but stick it out and make it work.*

FINDING FAMILY – *"Completing this series is like eating the last chip. Love Judith's writing and her female characters are always smart, strong, vulnerable to life and love experiences."*

"This was a refreshing book. Bringing the heart and soul of the family to us."

THE CHANDLER HILL INN SERIES – Books 1 – 3:

GOING HOME – *"I was completely immersed in this book, with the beautiful descriptive writing, and the author's way of bringing her characters to life. I felt like I was right inside her story."*

COMING HOME – *"Coming Home was such a wonderful story. The author has such a gift for getting the reader right to the heart of things."*

HOME AT LAST – "In this wonderful conclusion, to a heartfelt and emotional trilogy set in Oregon's stunning wine country, Judith Keim has tied up the Chandler Hill series with the perfect bow."

SEASHELL COTTAGE BOOKS:

A CHRISTMAS STAR – "Love, laughter, sadness, great food, and hope for the future, all in one book. It doesn't get any better than this stunning read."

CHANGE OF HEART – "CHANGE OF HEART is the summer read we've all been waiting for. Judith Keim is a master at creating fascinating characters that are simply irresistible. Her stories leave you with a big smile on your face and a heart bursting with love." ~Kellie Coates Gilbert, author of the popular Sun Valley Series

A SUMMER OF SURPRISES – "Ms. Keim uses this book as an amazing platform to show that with hard emotional work, belief in yourself, and love, the scars of abuse can be conquered. It in no way preaches, it's a lovely story with a happy ending."

A ROAD TRIP TO REMEMBER – "The characters are so real that they jump off the page. Such a fun, HAPPY book at the perfect time. It will lift your spirits and even remind you of your own grandmother. Spirited and hopeful Aggie gets a second chance at love and she takes the steering wheel and drives straight for it."

THE BEACH BABES – "Another winner at the pen of Judith Keim. I love the characters and the book just flows. It feels as though you are at the beach with them and are a part of you.

THE DESERT SAGE INN SERIES – Books 1 – 4:

THE DESERT FLOWERS – ROSE – *"The Desert Flowers - Rose, "In this first of a series, we see each woman come into her own and view new beginnings even as they must take this tearful journey as they slowly lose a dear friend.*

THE DESERT FLOWERS – LILY – *"The second book in the Desert Flowers series is just as wonderful as the first. Judith Keim is a brilliant storyteller. Her characters are truly lovely and people that you want to be friends with as soon as you start reading. Judith Keim is not afraid to weave real-life conflict and loss into her stories.*

THE DESERT FLOWERS – WILLOW – *"The feelings of love, joy, happiness, friendship, family, and the pain of loss are deeply felt by Willow Sanchez and her two cohorts Rose and Lily. The Desert Flowers met because of their deep feelings for Alec Thurston, a man who touched their lives in different ways."*

MISTLETOE AND HOLLY – *"As always, the author never ceases to amaze me. She's able to take characters and bring them to life in such a way that you think you're actually among family. It's a great holiday read. You won't be disappointed."*

THE SANDERLING COVE INN SERIES – Books 1 – 3:

WAVES OF HOPE – *"Such a wonderful story about several families in a beautiful location in Florida. A grandmother requests her three granddaughters to help her by running the family's inn for the summer. Other grandmothers in the area played a part in this plan to find happiness for their grandsons and granddaughters."*

SANDY WISHES – "Three cousins needing a change and a few of the neighborhood boys from when they were young are back visiting their grandmothers. It is an adventure, a summer of discoveries, and embracing the person they are becoming."

SALTY KISSES – "I love this story, as well as the entire series because it's about family, friendship, and love. The meddling grandmothers have only the best intentions and want to see their grandchildren find love and happiness. What grandparent wouldn't want that?"

THE LILAC LAKE INN SERIES – Books 1 – 3:

LOVE BY DESIGN –"Genie Wittner is planning on selling her beloved Lilac Inn B&B, and keeping a cottage for her three granddaughters, Whitney, the movie star, Dani an architect, and Taylor a writer. A little mystery, a possible ghost, and romance all make this a great read and the start of a new series."

LOVE BETWEEN THE LINES – "Taylor is one of 3 sisters who have inherited a cottage in Lilac Lake from their grandmother. She is an accomplished author who is having some issues getting inspired for her next book. Things only get worse when she receives an email from her new editor with a harsh critique of her last book. She's still fuming when Cooper shows up in town, determined to work together on getting the book ready."

LOVE UNDER THE STARS – "Love Under the Stars is the third book in The Lilac Lake Inn Series by author Judith Keim. Judith beautifully weaves together the final story in this amazing series about the Gilford sisters and their *grandmother, GG."*

THE LILAC LAKE BOOKS

LOVE'S CURE – *Welcome back to Lilac Lake with a new spin-off series from author Judith Keim. For fans of the author, you will be reunited with previous characters, as well as being introduced to new ones. Even though this book can be read as a stand-alone, I highly recommend reading the Lilac Lake Inn series to get introduced to all of these amazing characters.*

Love's Match

A Lilac Lake Book

by

Judith Keim

Wild Quail Publishing

Published in the United States of America by:

Wild Quail Publishing
PO Box 171332
Boise, ID 83717-1332

ISBN 978-1-965622-23-0

Dedication

This book is dedicated to foster parents everywhere.

CHAPTER ONE

FEELING LIKE A NAUGHTY CHILD, HAZEL BELMONT SAT IN the principal's office at the Emerson Wittner Elementary school where she taught third grade. It couldn't be good news. Nolan Deere wasn't the easiest man to get along with, and she'd had her disagreements with him during the past school year in the small town of Lilac Lake.

If she was about to lose her job as she suspected, she didn't want to lie in order to remain in New Hampshire as she wanted. Her mother had all but demanded she come home to New Orleans to marry a man chosen for her by their two conspiring mothers. A man she had no intention of marrying.

"Hazel? Mr. Deere will see you now," said the office secretary.

Hazel stood and automatically swiped at her pants to make sure they were straightened. Then she headed into the office where Nolan sat, a massive figure behind his desk. His size alone wasn't the only reason pupils tended to fall quickly in line. He usually wore a threatening scowl. Hazel had never let that affect her, which is one reason they seemed to clash often over small details.

"Well, Ms. Belmont, we've made it through the school year and, overall, things have gone okay. I'm sure you've heard, though, that student enrollment has gone down, and we'll be reducing third-grade classes from three to two, which leaves me with the unpleasant task of transferring a teacher. Because you were the last to arrive at my school, you are the teacher who will be asked to leave or be asked to teach at another school in our district. I'm sorry."

Hazel sat quietly, her mind racing. She loved her students, but she didn't love teaching. It was a draining, challenging job that didn't fulfill her as much as she thought it would. The growing demands made upon her and the other teachers itched like a black fly bite in the spring. She'd worked within the system, but now, thinking of being free to do something else, she knew what she must do.

"Thank you. It's been a most interesting year, and I love my students, but I think this might be an opportunity for me to do something else." The minute Hazel spoke the words, she felt a huge burden lift from her shoulders. She knew she'd done an excellent job. But it was just that. A job. Not a profession, as it was for many teachers like her best friend, Misty Owen, who taught at the same school.

Nolan's eyebrows shot up. "I don't mean you weren't an acceptable teacher. Your students love you, and the other teachers do too."

"I know," Hazel said, pleased that in another couple of weeks, she wouldn't have to deal with him. Or so many mandates. Or parents who wouldn't listen. Or endless evenings of correcting papers.

"Ms. Belmont, Hazel, we'll be sorry to lose you," said Nolan. "Please understand that this is an uncomfortable situation for me."

Hazel forced a pleasant expression. As usual, Nolan was backpedaling as fast as he could lest he be charged with something unpleasant.

"May I go now?" she asked.

"Certainly, certainly," said Nolan. "The district will send you the necessary paperwork."

"Thank you," Hazel said, standing.

They shook hands.

Hazel left the office, wondering if she'd made the correct choice. But when she turned back and saw Nolan watching her, she knew she was right. Now, she had to move quickly to come up with another job, so her mother would have no reason to continue begging her to come home to a life she didn't want.

When Hazel walked outside, Misty was waiting by Hazel's car.

"How did it go?" Misty asked her. "Was it what you thought it might be?"

"More or less. The bottom line is that I'm quitting teaching. They're reducing the third-grade classes to two, and since I'm the last they hired, I'm the first to go."

Misty hugged her. "I'm sorry."

"Actually, I'm not. I know you love teaching, but I'd rather do something else. This is my chance to make that change. But I need to find another job in a hurry. If my mother thinks I'm doing nothing, I swear she'll drag me home."

"No one wants you to leave Lilac Lake," said Misty firmly. "Now, let's figure out what you can do." She snapped her fingers. "How about working for Ross Roberts at the Sports Center? He mentioned he and Mike Dawson might be looking for someone."

Hazel gave her an uncertain look. "What kind of work? Ross would be a dream to work for. Mike, not so much. He's such an entitled playboy."

"It's worth a call," said Misty. "It could be a real opportunity for you." She checked her watch. "I've promised to meet David at his house. I'll see you at Jake's later tonight."

"I miss having you live close to me, but Poppy is a special neighbor too," said Hazel. "And, of course, I'm happy for your engagement to David." David Graham and his father owned a successful landscaping business in town. He and Misty were a cute couple.

After Misty left, Hazel climbed into her car and drove to her cabin along the river. It sat in a small collection of renovated rental cabins spaced along the upper banks. She'd been lucky to find such a cute place to live. From there, she could walk into the center of town in a matter of minutes.

When she pulled into the small neighborhood, she waved to Sarah Miller and her two darling daughters and came to a stop in front of her cabin.

She sat in her car letting her mind settle. She adored living in Lilac Lake and vowed to be open-minded about asking Ross for a job. Many of her friends were either engaged or recently married, giving them a permanent home in this area. So far, she hadn't met any man who was a compatible match.

Before she could lose her courage, Hazel backed out of her driveway and headed to the new Sports Center in town. Ross Roberts and Mike Dawson were the major partners in this adventure. Both Ross and Mike were former professional athletes—Ross in baseball and Mike in tennis. Ross was also part-owner of the Lilac Lake Inn and was married to Melissa Hendrickson, a former local chef. Mike had traded in the grind of competition on the pro circuit for teaching tennis both in Florida and here in New Hampshire.

The red-brick Sports Center covered a huge tract of land just outside of the center of town and offered tennis courts, a baseball field, and training facilities, pickleball courts, basketball courts inside and out, an inside Olympic-size swimming pool, and a fantastic gym. It was unlike anything else in the region and was growing busier all the time.

Hazel got out of her car and went inside to the reception area. A male high school student was handling the front desk.

"Hi. Is Ross Roberts here?" Hazel asked hopefully.

"He's outside checking the batting cage," said the young man without looking up at her.

"Thanks." Hazel wended her way through the center realizing it was a much bigger operation than she'd thought.

Outside, Ross was checking the fencing around the batting cage when Hazel found him. He looked up at her approach. "Hi, Hazel. What's up?"

"I need to talk to you," Hazel said. "Is this a convenient time?"

Ross walked toward her in an uneven gait. With sandy hair, blue eyes, and a boyish smile, he had been a favorite player for the NY Yankees before a knee injury from a motorcycle accident took him out of the game.

"It was time for a break anyway. What can I do for you?" he asked Hazel.

She straightened and spoke eagerly. "I'd like to talk to you about a job. Do you have an opening here?"

His gaze settled on her. "Don't you teach at the elementary school?"

"I won't be there after the school year ends. I'm leaving the teaching arena rather than being placed elsewhere. Though I love the kids, I've realized teaching isn't what I want to do."

Ross nodded agreeably. "I'm glad you love kids because we handle a lot of them here. Let's go into my office to discuss this."

They walked inside to an unpretentious office that held two desks and chairs, file cabinets, shelving for trophies and memorabilia, and some comfortable leather side chairs.

"Have a seat," said Ross, indicating a chair in front of the desk where he sat. "Did you bring a resumé?"

"No, I didn't. I came here on the spur of the moment at Misty's suggestion. I don't even know what kind of work you might be hiring for," said Hazel, realizing how unprofessional she sounded.

"Tell me what you see as your strengths and what kind of work you do that would benefit us. And please don't be shy about it," said Ross.

Hazel drew a deep breath. "Okay. I'm very well organized with excellent follow-through. I worked as an Executive Assistant one summer while I was in college, and I'm good with details. I like kids and the freedom to do my job. I'm able to work without supervision."

"Was that an issue teaching?" Ross asked. "I've heard the principal is difficult to get along with."

"He certainly was with me. He found every excuse he could to criticize me. It would've been comical if it hadn't become such a waste of time for everyone," admitted Hazel.

"That's too bad. I've been in a similar situation. Mike is due to arrive from Florida with a co-worker, a woman who will be teaching tennis with him. I have an idea I want to discuss with him, and then I'll get back in touch with you. How does that sound?"

"That would be wonderful," said Hazel. "I can be flexible and am willing to work hard at anything you need. I play tennis but haven't played much since college when I was on the tennis team. But I might be able to help. My hours can be flexible as well."

"Let me work on a couple of ideas. You'd want a full-time job with no summers off?"

"Yes. I'm looking for full-time work with benefits," Hazel said.

Ross gave her an understanding look. "Got it. I'll call you after Mike gets here, and we've had a chance to talk. Thanks for coming in." He stood.

Hazel rose and shook his hand, which quickly covered her much smaller one. "How's Melissa's cookbook coming along?"

Ross grinned. "It's a real chore testing recipes."

Hazel laughed. One reason she loved Lilac Lake so much was because it was filled with such interesting people her age.

Back home, Hazel poured herself a glass of iced tea and took it out to the back deck, which overlooked woods and farther down, the river. She needed time to reassess herself.

Sitting in a chair, she gazed out at the woods, enjoying the sunshine on her face. She hoped she'd done the right thing by turning down a transfer to another school. She was stubborn and could be quick to act. But her gut was usually right.

The one thing she knew for sure was that she didn't want to return to her hometown outside of New Orleans. God knew she loved the food there, and she loved her family, but she felt more alive here in the Lakes Region of New Hampshire where mountains, rivers, lakes, and adventure beckoned. It was a tight-knit town where people were comfortable in jeans, boots, and fleece jackets. Where women didn't use a lot of makeup, just a little lip gloss.

Hazel knew she was attractive; she'd often been told she was beautiful. But she didn't want to think of herself in those shallow terms. Looks fade. Instead, as she'd wanted to hear from Nolan Deere, she hoped to be thought of as creative, energetic, and fun.

Her mother told her she needed to be ladylike to be able to attract a good man. But she knew that belief was an archaic thought by which her mother and grandmother had been raised. It was laughable. At least to Hazel, who was named after that same proper grandmother.

Hazel went inside. She'd acted spontaneously by going to see Ross without a resume. Time to change that.

She sat at her desk in her small office and started to type up a list of all the jobs she'd held both during and after college. Though she came from a family where money wasn't an issue, earning it had always pleased her.

When her cell rang, Hazel picked it up. *Misty.*

"Hi," said Misty. "I just want to make sure you'll be at Jake's. I know that Melissa and Ross will be there. Maybe you can talk to Ross about a job opportunity."

"I have already talked to Ross," said Hazel, "and I think

there might be something at the Sports Center for me. He has to talk to Mike first, and then he'll get in touch with me. I was very encouraged."

"Mike should have no problem with you working there, even after a date that didn't go anywhere."

"He's nice, but I have the feeling he's a playboy. A bunch of groupies are always hanging around him in their little tennis skirts and shorts," said Hazel.

"You've got to admit he's a hottie if there ever was one. That ripped body, crooked smile, and those green eyes of his. Any woman would fall for him."

"Yes, but he seems to play them all, going from one to the other," said Hazel. "Even now he's bringing a co-worker, a woman, to Lilac Lake to help with the tennis program."

"Well, that'll make it easy for everyone," said Misty. "No competition from anyone here."

"Thanks for thinking of me," said Hazel. "I need to finish typing up my resumé before I take off for Jake's. I'll see you there."

Hazel ended the call. She hoped Misty was right and working with Mike wouldn't be a problem. There was something about him that annoyed her no end.

CHAPTER TWO

HAZEL DECIDED TO WALK TO JAKE'S BAR AND GRILL ON Main Street just a few blocks away. This was another pleasure of living in a small town.

She headed out. As she strolled along the sidewalk, she admired the colorful flowers people had planted in their front yards, placed in pots by the front door, or in baskets hanging from hooks on the front porch. Some of the houses flew the American flag, giving a real small-town feel to the setting.

On Main Street, she studied the cluster of intriguing shops and enticing restaurants. The town took pride in keeping to its reputation of being postcard-pretty.

The shops displayed different-colored awnings, many of them purple. Beside each door, at least one pot held flowers. The decorative lampposts along the street held baskets of petunias and other summer flowers. She passed Pages Bookstore, Poppy Browning's Wild Flower Boutique, Petals Flower Shop, and other retail establishments whose windows held interesting displays. Across the street, Bullard's Hardware Store filled the entire corner.

Jake's sat midway down Main Street and was where Hazel and her friends gathered at least a couple times a week to relax and catch up on the latest news. Two tables were usually reserved for them in the back corner, where they had some privacy from the tourists who came to Lilac Lake year-round.

Tonight, Hazel was one of the last people to arrive. She greeted everyone and placed an order for a cold beer and a chicken Caesar salad, catching the waitress before she left the table.

"How is everyone?" she asked brightly.

"The real question is how are you doing?" asked Whitney, one of the three Gilford sisters whose grandmother used to own the Lilac Lake Inn. "I heard from a neighbor that you won't be teaching at the elementary school next year."

"Nothing is secret for long in this town," grumbled Hazel. "But I suppose it's just as well to get the news out there. Instead of being transferred to another school, I decided to leave teaching." She glanced at Ross, who grinned at her. "I'm looking for other work. Something that will keep me here in Lilac Lake."

"We certainly don't want you leaving," said Whitney, looking wide-eyed.

Hazel held up a hand to stop such a notion. "Even though my parents want me to come home, I have no intention of leaving here. I love Lilac Lake."

"I'm relieved," said Dani Collister, Whitney's sister. "We need a touch of southern girl here." It had taken them a while to get used to Hazel's drawl, which appeared pronounced when she was especially flustered.

"Okay, y'all, I do declare all y'all are sweet as pah," said Hazel with exaggeration.

Everyone laughed.

Hazel's food came, and she sat quietly enjoying it and the conversation around her. Misty was telling everyone about fixing up the cabin where David lived. "We know that we'll eventually move into his parents' house by the lake, but the cabin is perfect for us now."

"It's not luxurious like Aaron's cabin," said David, "but it's comfortable."

Hazel turned to Sarah, Aaron Collister's fiancée. "How are things going with you and the girls living there?"

"It's a perfect place for all of us, including the dogs. Sometime this summer, we hope to have a party there," said Sarah, looking to Aaron for approval. "We'll have to see."

"That sounds wonderful," said Hazel, hoping she would still be living in Lilac Lake. She glanced at Ross, and he winked at her.

Conversation turned to Melissa's cookbook, and Hazel relaxed. Everyone in town knew what a creative chef Melissa had been at her parents' restaurant before it burned down. Hazel could well imagine how outstanding the cookbook would be.

"How's the hardware store doing?" Hazel asked Dani. She'd recently bought a share of the business and was working with Sarah, whose parents had started the store years ago.

"It's very exciting," said Dani. "I'm dealing with the construction and renovation areas of the store while Sarah is handling gifts and housewares."

Brad put his arm around Dani. "I like to see you settled and doing what you want."

Watching them, Hazel felt a ping of envy. She knew she didn't need a man to make her happy, but that didn't mean she wouldn't like a special one in her life.

A few days later, Hazel was sitting in her classroom

correcting math papers when Nolan Deere knocked on her door and entered the room.

"Ms. Belmont, it seems there's been an increase in enrollment. I've received many calls from your students' parents requesting you to teach their siblings. I'd like you to remain at our school." He stood beside her desk, looking down at her with an unpleasant expression.

"I don't know what to say," said Hazel, both delighted and furious with his request. She hadn't heard from Ross and wondered whether Mike would be willing to hire her. He already knew she was never going to be a groupie of his.

"Just say yes, and we'll forget the whole ... firing thing ... misunderstanding ... happened," said Nolan.

Wait a minute! Firing thing? "Well, now that I've had a moment to think about it, I'll say thanks, but no thanks. I have other plans."

"Other plans? But it's only been a couple of days ..."

"Enough for me to decide to make those changes I was forced to consider," said Hazel, calmly but firmly. "Now, I'm pleased to explore other opportunities."

"Like what?" Nolan sneered.

"That's really none of your concern," Hazel said, forcing herself to hold her temper in check.

"All right. You've had your chance," said Nolan. He turned on his heel and left the room in a huff.

Hazel watched him go and then sat back in her chair, satisfied. Some days were full of surprises. She just hoped bad news from Ross wouldn't ruin her decision.

On the way out of school, Hazel met up with Misty.

"Do you have time for a cup of coffee at my house?" Hazel asked her. "I want to make sure I haven't been a fool because of my pride."

Misty gave her a questioning look. "Sure. I've got time. It sounds important."

They each drove to the cabins and parked in front of Hazel's home.

Hazel unlocked her front door and waved Misty inside. "Sorry, it's been a busy week, so it's kind of messy. But let me get the coffee going, and we can sit outside on the deck. It's such a perfect time of year to do that."

"I miss my cabin here along the river," said Misty. "But I love being with David. He's easy-going, and we have a lot of fun. After living together for a while, it's fantastic to know we're compatible."

"Nothing like seeing a roomie in the morning for several weeks to know what they're really like," said Hazel, fixing them each a cup of coffee.

Misty laughed. "David gets up very early for work. Sometimes, I don't."

They walked out to the deck and sat down.

Misty leaned forward and faced Hazel with a look of concern. "What's going on?"

Hazel told her about Nolan's visit to her classroom. "He was shocked that I said no thanks after he reluctantly admitted enrollment has increased and parents have been requesting me for the next school year. I'm glad I'd already made up my mind to do something different. Even if parents want me to stay."

"Believe me, no one else wanted you to leave," said Misty.

"I've grown to dislike even the sight of Nolan Deere. He's so insincere. He didn't look very happy about offering me my job back."

"He's not an easy person to get along with," said Misty. "I tend to stay out of his way. There's been talk of his transferring to another school. If that happens, I can't think of any teacher who'd miss him."

"I'm glad it isn't just me who can't seem to get along with him. I like to think I can deal with most people," said Hazel.

Misty took another sip of her coffee and set her mug down on the table between them. "You're a fabulous teacher. It's a shame that Nolan has made you think about leaving. But I get it, if you want to try something else. You know you can count on me for a reference."

"Thanks," said Hazel. "I just needed to talk to you about it to make sure I wasn't being stupid."

Misty laughed. "One thing you're not is stupid. I'm sure you have some exciting times ahead. I just don't want you to leave town."

"Me neither," said Hazel. "I'm dreading a call from my mother until I can safely say I've already got another job."

"Has Ross offered you a job?" asked Misty.

"Not yet, but I think he will. I just hope it's something that can give me the same benefits as teaching. Other than that, I'll be fine. Have you made plans for the summer?"

"David and I were talking about that earlier this week. I was going to take a summer course, but instead, I'm going to spend time with his mother, learning about the business end of the landscaping company. While the staff is busy working outside, I can take over the indoor plant business they have, taking care of plants in offices and professional buildings in the entire region."

"I'm afraid I'd kill all the plants," said Hazel.

"I'm learning a lot about them. Each variety of plant has certain requirements. Believe me, I'm still checking my notes," Misty admitted.

"You and David make such a sweet couple. Thanks for listening to me."

"Anytime," said Misty, checking her watch. "I've got to be going, but I'm always here to support you."

They hugged, and Hazel showed Misty out, then returned to the deck to collect the mugs. She hoped by the time the gang met at Jake's over the weekend, Ross would have good news for her.

CHAPTER THREE

WHEN HAZEL WALKED INTO JAKE'S ON SATURDAY NIGHT, she felt a little jittery. She'd heard Mike was back in town, and she was hoping for an indication that he and Ross had reached a positive decision about a job offer.

She went to the back tables reserved for her and her friends and saw Ross and Melissa sitting with Mike and a dark-haired beauty, along with some other group members.

Ross looked up, saw her, and waved her over to a chair next to him, across from Mike.

She greeted everyone and sat down.

"I'm glad you could make it," said Ross. "As you can see, Mike is back in town. And this is Tracy Rodriguez. She's going to be working in our tennis program this summer."

Tracy smiled at her. "Hi, I'm with Mike."

Amused by how Tracy had staked her claim on him, Hazel held out her hand. "Nice to meet you."

As they shook hands, Hazel noted how strong Tracy's fingers were and realized how fit she was.

More people arrived, and Hazel resigned herself to the fact that there would be no job discussion in this setting. She turned to Dani and began talking to her about the hardware store.

Because it was the weekend, people stayed longer than on some nights. By the time the group began to break up, Hazel was more than ready to go home.

As she walked out of the restaurant, Ross caught up with her. "Come see us tomorrow. We can talk. How does two o'clock sound?"

Hazel heaved a sigh of relief. "Perfect. Thanks. I'll see you then."

As he left, Whitney came up beside Hazel. "You've got an interview with Ross? I know how much you want this."

"I've been pretty open about not wanting to return to teach under Nolan Deere. Hopefully, there's a job for me at the Sports Center."

"If that doesn't work out, I'm sure we can all help you find a job somewhere in town," said Whitney, giving her an encouraging pat on the back.

Hazel went to her car and climbed in, feeling optimistic.

The next morning, Hazel sipped coffee and nibbled on a piece of toast as she sat in front of her computer researching the Sports Center. Their website was very helpful, showing a map of the layout of the entire project. Ross Roberts and Mike Dawson were the majority owners with a few other investors. Very little was said about them on the website, but Hazel looked them up online.

She knew a lot about Ross's background, growing up in New Jersey and playing baseball since he was a kid. He'd been a standout all his sporting life. Now, he was married to Melissa Hendrickson and living in Lilac Lake. Ross was easy-going and open as he made friends in town.

Mike was another story. He was a Florida state champion in tennis who'd gone professional, had grown up in northern Florida, and had run a tennis camp year-round for several years. The facts about him were pretty lean. Mike didn't live in Lilac Lake, and though he was pleasant to everyone when he was visiting, he was guarded when it came to talking about himself.

Mike and she had dated one time, but Hazel lost any interest when she realized Mike had a female friend in Florida. Though she and Mike saw each other from time to time, they kept their distance. Now, she was in a difficult position because she needed his support to be able to work at the Sports Center.

As Hazel dressed for the interview, her instinct was not to fuss too much with her appearance. She doubted any job at the Sports Center would require more than very casual clothing. On the other hand, her training and her pride made her do her best with her hair, use a little makeup, and put on her favorite pair of slacks and a bright, floral, summer sweater.

She carried a leather folder containing two copies of her revised resumé. This updated version listed some of the work she'd done before she began her teaching career—things like the summer she worked as an administrative assistant, and the summer she worked at a children's camp.

Hazel drove to the Sports Center, parked, and got out, interested to see some activity on the baseball field. She went to the main entrance and spoke to the person behind the reception desk. A pretty young girl who wore a T-shirt with the high school logo on it.

"I have an appointment with Ross Roberts," she said. "I'm Hazel Belmont."

The girl looked down at some paperwork on the desk. "Oh, I see a note here that says you're to meet with Mike Dawson in the office." She gave Hazel a quick smile. "You're lucky. The office is to your right, first door on the right."

"Thanks. I know," said Hazel, feeling her fingers grow cold. Just her luck. Ross wouldn't be there to support her.

Hazel walked down the corridor rehearsing pleasant things to say.

When she got to the office door, she knocked.

"Come in," said a deep voice from inside.

Hazel opened the door and stared at Mike, who was talking on the phone. At his indication, she sat in a leather chair facing his desk.

"Okay, gotta go," said Mike. "I'll talk to you later." He hung up the phone and stood, showing off his trim, muscular, sun-kissed body that would make any woman between the ages of twelve and ninety-two drool. His light-streaked brown hair was pulled back into a ponytail. But it was his green eyes that captured her as the corners of them crinkled from the smile on his handsome face.

"Well, Hazel, I was surprised when Ross told me you were interested in working here. Let's talk about that."

Hazel had felt uncomfortable in the principal's office. This was even worse.

Gathering herself, Hazel said, "Hi, Mike. I understand that you're back in Lilac Lake at least for the summer."

"Yes. It was nice to be able to leave Florida's summer heat and come here."

Hazel handed him her resumé. "This will explain some of my qualifications."

He took the paper and set it down on his desk without looking at it. "I heard you quit teaching. Why?"

"It wasn't a matter of quitting. The principal needed to find a new home for one of his third-grade teachers, and because I was the last hired, he told me he'd have no room for me in the coming year. Rather than move to a different school, I chose to leave."

"That sounds pretty straightforward. Won't you miss the kids? I thought you liked teaching," Mike said.

"I do and I don't. I certainly didn't like working for Nolan Deere, the principal. He and I had different ideas about teaching methods. It became a sort of sick joke."

He studied her. "Why would you choose to work at the Sports Center?"

"Actually, Misty Owens suggested I look into it. She'd heard Ross was looking for someone to help out."

He shrugged. "Fair enough. What kind of help can you offer us?"

"If you look at my resumé, you'll see that besides working with people of all ages, I can do administrative work. I enjoy helping a business run smoothly. I did that one summer in college as an assistant and liked it. But my parents wanted me to get my teaching degree, and it seemed like the wise thing to do, a worthy profession and all that."

Mike's gaze settled on her. "But if you worked in an administrative capacity here, you'd have to accept taking orders from both Ross and me. How would that work?"

Hazel twitched in her seat and then straightened. "I've never had a problem teaching or working for anyone before dealing with Nolan. It's a personality clash. He even asked me to come back to teaching, when there was an increase in enrollment."

"So, why aren't you back?" asked Mike.

Hazel sighed and decided to speak the truth. "Haven't you ever had a moment when you knew that a change in your life was the right thing? As soon as I was forced to look at what my life was like, I knew I wanted to try something new. This was an opportunity, not a loss."

Mike's lips curved. "Sort of like lemons and lemonade?"

Hazel returned his smile. "I guess you could say that. At any rate, I'm excited about the chance to work at the Sports Center. I've been reading about it online and speaking to Ross. It seems you could use someone to handle the administrative facets of the business, so you and Ross have time to work with your students."

Mike sat back in his chair and gave her a thoughtful look. "What would you do or change?"

"Okay, I've thought about this and will be honest with you. I think the person at the front desk should be wearing one of the Center's T-shirts, make no personal comments about other staff, and take the effort to show visitors to their proper locations. It was just a quick observation."

"We're really casual here," said Mike, a little defensively.

"I don't see anything wrong with that, but a matter of training can go a long way. I think it's smart to hire high school students. This is a community setting, and though I understand the Center is for the benefit of the entire region, I like the idea of presenting a positive image of Lilac Lake's participation."

Mike just stared at her.

Hazel stopped talking, realizing she might have sounded too forceful about it.

"Are you always so enthusiastic about your job?" Mike asked.

"I try to be," Hazel said, thinking she'd blown it.

"Let me look over your resume, talk to Ross, and he'll get back to you," said Mike. "He's busy with a baseball clinic, or he would've been here."

He rose, and Hazel followed.

"Thank you for coming in." Mike flashed her a wicked grin. "Can you find your way out?"

Feeling her cheeks grow warm, she said, "I think I can manage."

She left, unsure of how the interview went.

Instead of going home to sit and wonder about it alone, Hazel went to the Lilac Café for a late lunch. If Jake's was the place where people in her crowd went in the evening, the Café was the place where they met during the day.

Hazel parked the car and went inside. Several people were sitting inside in booths or at tables. She checked the patio and saw an empty table outside.

As she stepped onto the patio, she noticed Taylor Gilford Walker and her husband, Cooper, sitting outside talking to an unfamiliar man.

Taylor saw her and waved her over. "Come sit with us."

Glad for the company, Hazel walked over and joined them.

"This is Henrik Larsen, Cooper's lawyer," said Taylor. "He's in town for a work visit, but we're hosting a party for him tonight at the cottage. I hope you'll come. We're sending out last-minute invitations."

"It sounds delightful," said Hazel.

"Have a seat," said Cooper. "We just ordered." He waved a waitress over to them.

Hazel ordered her favorite chicken salad and a glass of iced tea and then sat back.

"Henrik, this is Hazel Belmont, a transplanted southern belle from New Orleans," teased Cooper.

"Now, Coopah, y'all know that's a bit of exaggeration," said Hazel, playing along.

The newcomer was a handsome man who looked to be in his late forties or early fifties. He had light-brown hair going gray at the temples, beautiful blue eyes, and rosy cheeks that went well with his quick smile.

"I'm pleased to meet you," said Henrik. "What do you do in town?"

"At the moment, I'm not sure. I'm a third-grade teacher who may be moving on to something else," said Hazel. "If you're Cooper's lawyer, do you live in New York City?"

"Yes, but when I got the chance to carry on business here, I quickly accepted, eager to see the town I've heard so much about."

"I love living here," said Hazel. "It takes some getting used to the quirks of small-town living where everyone knows your business, but I'm at home here."

"As exciting as New York City is, I like being part of both worlds," said Taylor.

"I'm finding myself here more than there. As long as I can do my job anywhere, this is where I want to be. Of course, some of my work has to be done in the city," said Cooper.

Their food came, and conversation was intermittent as they enjoyed their meal. At the end of it, Hazel politely excused herself with the promise to bring some of her fudge brownies to the party.

At home, pleased to have something to fill her afternoon as she waited for a phone call from Ross, she got out the ingredients for her brownies.

When she hadn't heard from Ross by the time she was ready to leave for the party, she told herself that no news wasn't necessarily bad news and headed out.

CHAPTER FOUR

The Lilac Lake Cottage was part of the property excluded from the sale of the Lilac Lake Inn the Gilford women's grandmother, GG, Genie Wittner, had owned. She'd arranged with the buyers for her family to retain the cottage and a few acres around it, with the understanding that the cottage would be renovated and lived in at least six months of the year.

Though there was room for all three sisters to stay there, it was mostly Taylor, or Taylor and Cooper, who lived there because Whitney and Dani were married and living in town already.

On this May afternoon, the weather cooperated with a sunny, pleasant day.

Hazel parked her car, got out, and carefully carried her tray of brownies and a bottle of wine to share. Walking toward the house, she caught up to Poppy Browning and Blake Loomis.

"Good afternoon," said Hazel, smiling at them.

"A lovely day for a party," said Blake. He gave Poppy a meaningful look.

Poppy held out her left hand so Hazel could see the gorgeous diamond sitting on her ring finger.

"Oh, Poppy! I'm so excited for you and Blake! Congratulations! As soon as I get rid of what I'm carrying, I'll give you a hug," cried Hazel.

Blake put an arm around Poppy. "She's made me a happy man."

"You guys are perfect together," said Hazel, making room for Whitney and Nick Woodruff to join them.

Whitney and Nick commented on the engagement, and Hazel eased away. She was ecstatic for Poppy, who in her early forties had all but given up on finding the man she wanted to marry. This would be Blake's second marriage, and this union couldn't happen to a nicer guy.

Hazel's excitement faded as she realized that everyone else seemed to be moving ahead with a new love. She reminded herself of the importance of staying strong, not falling for someone she knew she wouldn't be content with for the long haul.

She walked into the kitchen to deliver her gifts and found Mike with Tracy, the beautiful woman he'd been with last night.

"Hi, Mike. Hi, Tracy. It's so nice to see such a crowd here."

Tracy didn't say anything. Mike gave Hazel a quick grin and moved away, Tracy trailing behind him.

Hazel's self-confidence took a beating. She told herself that this wasn't the place to discuss business and that it was in her best interest to stay away from them. For some reason, she didn't think Tracy liked her.

Misty and David walked into the kitchen, and soon Hazel and Misty joined a group of female friends.

Time flew as the party grew bigger and louder, and more food was offered.

By the time Hazel headed home, she wasn't worrying about her job at the Sports Center. She had a lot of people behind her. She'd get the job or not.

At school the next day, Hazel looked out over her class and felt a pang of regret that she wouldn't continue to follow their progress in school. All of them mattered to her.

Nolan Deere stuck his head into her classroom, walked over to her, and said quietly, "Are you sure you won't change your mind about staying?"

Feeling as if fate were calling to her, she nodded.

Grimacing, he left the room.

Hazel wasn't sure what the future would bring. She just knew it was time for things to change. Wasn't that what life was all about—taking chances and meeting new challenges?

Hazel was packing up school papers to take home when her cell phone rang. *Ross.*

"Hi," said Hazel, unable to hide the note of hope in her voice.

"Mike and I are wondering if you can stop at the Sports Center on your way home," said Ross. "We want to talk to you about a position here."

"Excellent. I'm just about to leave school. I'll see you shortly," said Hazel calmly, though her heart was pumping blood through her at an alarming pace.

She ended the call and did a little dance by her desk, thanking her lucky stars she hadn't been wrong about moving forward. She stopped suddenly, hoping she wasn't being premature. She had no idea what the job was.

Hazel hurried to her car and took off for the Center,

pleased she wouldn't have to wait long to find out.

She went inside the Center and was satisfied to see that the high school student behind the desk was wearing a Sports Center T-shirt.

"May I help you?" the student asked her.

"I'm here to meet with Ross Roberts and Mike Dawson," Hazel replied.

"Oh, yes. Let me show you to their office," said the student.

Hazel didn't have the heart to tell her she knew the way and dutifully followed her.

When she knocked on the door and opened it, both men stood.

"Glad you're here," said Ross. "Mike and I have been discussing how best to use you for support. Please, have a seat." He indicated the leather chair in front of his desk.

Mike pulled up the other leather chair, and they sat in a circle.

"Ross and I are used to setting up our own classes and private lessons," said Mike. "But we need someone to handle other details for us."

"And someone to run the front office, so to speak," said Ross. "In other words, someone to run the Center. We need someone willing to work all jobs from receptionist to helping camp counselors, to typing up schedules, to working on promotional material."

"You won't be involved with the financial end of things. We've hired an accountant for that," said Mike. "He's someone who will handle all the forms, reports, and payments required to operate a facility like ours with reporting responsibilities to the city, county, and state."

"But the details of running the administration would be in your hands," said Ross. "You'd have to be willing to be flexible and fulfill our requests, whether you agree with them or not," said Ross, giving her a steady look.

Hazel's cheeks grew warm. "I assure you, I can do that."

"Good," said Mike. "But we want you to feel free to speak up when you see a need for improvement. I hope you noticed the changes at the reception desk."

Hazel grinned. "I did. And I thought it was a commendable way to greet guests."

"So do we," said Ross, giving her a thumbs up. "Now for the salary and benefits. The benefits are about the same as you were getting." He handed her a piece of paper with everything printed out for her to see.

Hazel let out a breath of relief as she went over the numbers. "This is certainly fair. I hope to prove that I'm even more valuable to you."

Ross laughed. "I like that response. I know you have a couple more weeks of school, but I'm hoping you will be able to work for us on the weekends as we get camps and classes scheduled."

"Tracy will handle my private student sessions for me, setting up a schedule and assisting me," said Mike. "She will head the tennis camp for kids. Ross tells me you've played tennis on a high school team. Perhaps we can use your help with the camp. We'll see."

Hazel nodded agreeably, though she privately hoped she wouldn't have to work with Tracy.

Ross stood. "Well, then, we'll have you fill out the

employment paperwork and return it to us as soon as possible. Congratulations, Hazel. Welcome aboard." He shook her hand.

Then it was Hazel's turn to shake hands with Mike.

His fingers gripped her hand, sending a stream of nervous energy up the length of her arm. At least, that's how she was willing to accept the sensations that shot through her. The last thing she wanted was to get involved with someone at work. She knew how that went.

Hazel left the center and went directly home to fill out the paperwork. The job was much more than what she'd hoped for, both in scope and salary. She knew she'd be busy but felt secure about doing the job, even if it meant she'd have little time for anything else this summer.

After she'd completed filling out the papers, Hazel poured herself a glass of pinot noir and took it out to the deck to celebrate. Sitting in the peaceful surroundings, Hazel felt a wave of relief wash over her. She had the perfect reason not to go home this summer, as her mother wanted.

Rather than wait for the weekend to do any work at the Sports Center, Hazel used the next couple of afternoons after school to walk through the Center, to see what was happening in various parts, and to check for postings on the bulletin board.

Hazel made a list of things she could do from home, and during the evenings there, she set up both weekly and monthly activity schedules to post.

She also started separate files for Ross and Mike, including listings of classes with names, addresses, and phone numbers of participants in their classes, and for individual classes.

On Saturday morning, Hazel brought in her computer to show Ross and Mike what she'd done so they would approve of her posting the schedules on the bulletin board and at the reception desk.

Ross wasn't there, but Mike was in his office with Tracy.

Hazel explained what she wanted to do and showed him her work.

He looked at it. "I'm impressed. This is the sort of thing that needs to be done."

Tracy shrugged. "I could've done that."

"I'll look around to see what else I can do to get things organized," said Hazel, anxious to leave his office.

"Thanks," said Mike.

Hazel tried not to notice the cold stare Tracy gave her and left, determined not to let anyone ruin her new job.

Though some degree of organization had been set up, Hazel found holes in those attempts. She discovered she loved the challenge of being in charge, overseeing the operation as one big whole instead of individual offerings, and smoothing arrangements so that everyone could easily see what was happening throughout the Center. When Hazel's last day at school arrived, she stood with the other teachers waving off their students. Some of the teachers had tears in their eyes. Hazel, like others, beamed at the idea of having a break from the draining schedule of teaching.

Misty wrapped an arm across her shoulder. "Guess this is it for you."

"It's going to be a busy summer, for sure."

"Have you told your mother about your new job?" asked Misty.

Hazel shook her head. "It hasn't come up, and I didn't want to say anything until I was officially on duty. But I owe her a phone call, and I'll tell her then. How about you? Are you enjoying working at the landscaping company?"

"Yes, though I don't see David much at all except in the evenings when he comes home from work. His mother is a delight, and I often wonder if this is what it must be like to have a real mother."

"Everyone knows she adores you," said Hazel. She knew her mother loved her, but they had very different ideas about what was important in life. Elliott Gladstone was part of that problematic situation. Her mother and his had planned for them to marry when they were just toddlers. They'd dated, but Hazel was very aware that he had no interest in her or any other woman. Their mothers, however, didn't have a clue.

Hazel and Misty hugged, and then Hazel went home to change into a pair of jeans and a red Sports Center T-shirt. On some people, they might look ordinary, but on Hazel's long shapely legs, the jeans looked especially attractive, and the T-shirt showed off her full breasts without being too obvious.

Mike and Ross were taking her to dinner at the Lilac Lake café.

When she walked into the café, Hazel saw Mike and Ross sitting at a table outside with another man.

Ross saw her and waved her over.

Hazel approached the table, studying the slim, nice-looking, brown-haired man wearing glasses, gesturing to Mike as he spoke.

All three men stood as she approached and settled into her chair.

"Hello," Hazel said, smiling at the three of them.

"Hazel, I'd like you to meet Craig Evans, our financial manager," said Ross. "He's just moved here from Boston. Craig, this is Hazel Belmont, the woman who's going to keep us organized. You two may want to set up some individual meetings to see how you can work together."

"Craig's a whiz at keeping track of the many filings we must do and catching spots where we can improve," said Mike.

"Do you give advice like a consultant?" Hazel asked Craig.

"I try to comment when I see things that need to be addressed," he said. "Things like pricing for classes and lessons. Where they might be increased or decreased for better participation."

"I like that. I have questions to ask you. For instance, I noticed the Center doesn't have a retail outlet where tennis rackets and gear, baseball mitts, and such can be sold. I bet the Concord sports store, Access Sports, might be interested in making a deal with the Center to sell things at the Center, with us getting a portion of the sales. Something like that."

All three men smiled at her.

Craig chuckled. "No wonder Ross and Mike are so pleased to have you on board. Great idea."

"There are ways to increase sales and participation at all times of the year by cooperating with the Inn for workout weekends and the like," said Hazel. "I worked with a nonprofit one summer, and there are all kinds of ways to make do through cooperative efforts."

"When I checked your references, the praise for your work was outstanding," said Ross. "Now, I see why."

He glanced at Mike.

"Yes, I think it's going to work out just fine," Mike said.

Hazel warmed to their praise, feeling she'd made the right choice by leaving teaching. She'd already decided she'd get her taste of being with kids by helping out at some of the summer camps they were offering.

A waitress came to their table, and they all ordered. Then Hazel sat back in her chair, content to participate in non-business talk.

"Where are you living?" she asked Craig.

"I'm renting a house in town from Blake Loomis," said Craig. "If I like it, I may buy it from him. He recently bought it to fix up."

"That sounds interesting. You'll love living in town," said Hazel. "Of course, small-town living has its quirks."

"I'm fine with any of it. I came out years ago and am comfortable with myself." He flashed her a smile that lit his dark eyes, and Hazel returned it. Craig seemed like a very nice man.

That evening, Hazel sat at her kitchen table making notes about the day's activities and what she intended to work on. She was pleased by the way Mike and Ross had encouraged her to do her own thing, only checking in with them when it was necessary.

Her cell phone rang. *Her mother.*

"Hi, Mom. I've been meaning to call you. I said I would, but time has slipped away. Let me tell you what I've been doing."

"I hope you're getting ready to come home and spend the summer with your father and me and, of course, Elliott."

"That's what I want to talk to you about," Hazel said. "I have a new job. I'm no longer teaching and have started working at the new Sports Center here in town. It's a much bigger operation than it sounds. They have every kind of sports facilities available, along with classes and children's camps. As you can imagine, summer is a very busy time for us."

"Whoa! Wait a minute. No longer teaching? What happened? You know how I feel about the importance of your teaching. It's so respectable."

"I agree, but the school needed to eliminate a third-grade teacher, and because I was hired last, I was the first to be let go. And as it so happened, I'm excited to be doing a different kind of work for more money and with the same benefits."

"Did you say Sports Center? What kind of job is there for you? You haven't played tennis since high school," her mother said testily.

"I'm their new administrator," Hazel said proudly. "It gives me a chance to use my organizational skills and a lot of creativity. I've just started, but I love it already."

"It might be an opportunity to meet a lot of young men there," said her mother. "Your cousin, Marla, has just announced she's having her second baby. Your aunt is ecstatic."

"Mom, you know I'm not ready to settle down, and

certainly not with Elliott." Hazel couldn't, wouldn't say why. It was up to Elliott to come out on his own. She'd do nothing to hurt him. He was kind and sweet to her.

"Do you have some man up there you're not telling me about?" her mother asked slyly.

"Yes," blurted Hazel, tired of this old game. Too late, she realized she might've made a bad choice.

"Oh, in that case, let me know when I can come visit and meet him. In the meantime, I think Elliott is planning to come to Lilac Lake. This way, he could see for himself. I'm so glad we had this chance to talk. Now, who is the lucky man to have your attention?"

Hazel froze. She needed to pick someone who had no interest in her but who might be willing to play along. She mentally raced through her list of single male friends and suddenly knew who that might be.

"His name is Mike. Mike Dawson."

"Excellent," said her mother. "Such a pleasant-sounding name. Now, tell me what he does."

"Mom, I'm not ready to talk about him," said Hazel firmly. "You don't want to jinx it, do you?"

"No, you're right. Just let me know when I can fly up there," said her mother. "Oops! Here's your father. He's taking me to dinner at the club. He says hello. You and I will talk later. Love you."

"Love you too," said Hazel, feeling sick at the thought of the lie she'd told her mother. It was sure to come back and bite her in the behind.

CHAPTER FIVE

WHEN **H**AZEL WENT INTO THE **C**ENTER THE NEXT DAY, she had every intention of speaking to Mike about her horrible predicament. But every time she went to the office at the opposite end of the corridor to hers, Tracy was with him.

By afternoon, Hazel was a wreck, holding it all inside.

She went to Mike's office, catching him there after he'd completed a private lesson.

Feeling her nerves perform a nervous tap dance, she knocked and went inside.

Mike lifted his head. "Hi, Hazel. What's up?"

"I need to talk to you about something," she began as Tracy entered the room.

"What's going on?" Tracy asked.

"I just needed to talk to Mike about something. Don't worry. I'll come back," Hazel said, realizing the situation had just gotten worse. If Tracy ever found out about the lie, she'd be furious. And Hazel wouldn't blame her. She knew Tracy was doing everything she could to hold Mike's attention.

She walked back to her own office at the end of the hallway and continued to set it up. The Center had given her a new computer, and she was in the process of transferring files and ideas to it.

She was still working on it when Mike knocked on the door. "You wanted to see me?"

Feeling her mouth go dry, Hazel nodded.

Mike stepped inside and gazed around. "Nothing fancy, but it's workable. I see you decided to add a couple of plants."

"Yes, I love them. They came from my classroom. One of them was given to me by a student."

Mike sat in one of the two wooden chairs and faced her. "So, what did you want to talk to me about?"

"I've done something terrible, all to get my mother off my back. She's an old-fashioned woman who's determined to see her daughter married and giving her grandchildren. Something I'm not ready to do." Hazel stopped and drew a deep breath to steady herself. This was so damn embarrassing.

"What does that have to do with me?" asked Mike.

"When I spoke to my mother last night, she pushed and pushed that idea until I guess I snapped. When she asked if I had a man in town that I wasn't telling her about, I lied to her. And when she pushed for a name, your name popped out."

"My name? Why me?" asked Mike, sitting up to attention.

"I knew it had to be someone who would never be interested in me. I'm not your type. I just need you to play along if my mother ever comes to town. Summertime is busy for her, so I don't expect her to come north anytime soon." Hazel crossed her cold fingers together, feeling sick as she gazed at him.

"Let me get this straight," said Mike. "You want me to pretend to be your boyfriend because you know that would never happen." He shrugged. "As long as we can keep it to a business agreement, I think I can do that."

"Please don't ever tell Tracy. She would be very unhappy with me," said Hazel, "and I don't want to cause any problems at work."

"I appreciate that," said Mike. "And the only time we have to pretend to be together is if your mother or someone else in your family visits. Is that right?"

Hazel bobbed her head; her throat was too clogged with tears of embarrassment to answer.

Mike got to his feet. "Well, then. That's taken care of. Ross and I have been thinking it's time for me to start lessons with you. Ross suggested you get up to speed with your game, so you can help with group tennis lessons for the younger groups."

"Okay," said Hazel, liking the idea. Anything to pay back Mike for his willingness to help her.

That afternoon, Hazel drove to Concord to visit Access Sports. Not only did she need to talk to them about a cooperative deal, but Hazel also needed some tennis clothes and a new tennis racket. Her old racket was usable, but if she was going to be a support to some of the clinics, she wanted a newer one.

When she arrived at the store, it was even better than she'd heard about. The women's section had tennis clothes to suit every style and size, and a complete section for pickleball.

She was wandering through the selection when a well-built young man approached her. "Can I help you?"

"Right now, I'm browsing, but I'm interested in a couple of outfits, and I want to get a new racket. I might as well get a pickleball paddle, too. First, I'd like to talk to the manager."

"I'm Tom Jeffries, the assistant manager. My father owns the store. How can I help you?"

"I'm Hazel Belmont, the new Administrator at the Sports Center in Lilac Lake. I'd like to discuss a merchandising arrangement with you."

His eyes lit. "A couple of months ago, I called there, hoping to talk to the owners about doing business with them. Come into my office. My father is out, but we can work on structuring a deal for all to approve."

Pleased, Hazel followed Tom into his office, which contained samples of outfits strewn on a table and a box of blue baseball hats with a logo Hazel didn't recognize. Shelves in his office contained several trophies.

"Oh, I see you're a wrestler," said Hazel. "Wow! A state champion."

"That was my sport," said Tom. "Now, I coach the high school team." He indicated a chair. "Please sit down. I'm anxious to hear what you have in mind."

Hazel lowered herself into a chair and removed some papers from her purse. "This is a list of ideas I had for how we can cooperate. The Center doesn't have a retail outlet yet, but both Ross Roberts and Mike Dawson agree we should have one. Until we add that, I think we can display some items from your store on the wall behind the reception desk and in the main entrance."

"And you'd do that because ..." Tom said smiling.

"Because we'd get a percentage of the sales through the center. In addition, we'd offer our clients special offers to your store, again for a percentage of sales. The Center is drawing people from all over for a variety of sports. It could be a very smart arrangement for both of us."

"I agree," said Tom. "I can come to the Center and help

you devise a retail area there. Let me talk to my father and then come meet with you and the owners there." He stood. "This is a fabulous plan. I have you to thank for it, Hazel. Now, let's take care of what you need."

Pleased, Hazel followed Tom into the store, picked out a racket, and tried on several outfits before choosing a skirt, shorts, two different tops, and a jacket, all interchangeable.

It was a big investment for her, so she was excited when Tom gave her an employee discount.

"Whoever selects women's clothing has done a fabulous job," said Hazel.

"That would be my wife, Evie," said Tom, waving an attractive blonde over to them at the checkout desk.

After introductions were made and the two women had chatted for a while, Hazel invited her to visit the Center.

"I'd love to see it," said Evie. "When I heard that Mike Dawson was the tennis pro, I decided that, somehow, I'd make time for a private lesson or two. He could've stayed on the circuit and decided not to. He's that talented."

Hazel had never heard the story, but now she began to wonder about Mike's life before coming to Lilac Lake.

She said goodbye to Tom and Evie and left with Tom's promise to come to the Center soon with her new tennis racket strung especially for her.

After bundling her purchases into her car, she drove to Office Depot to pick up supplies that were already approved by Ross. In addition to completing her own office, Hazel was helping Craig set up his office and buying supplies for all aspects of running the center. Paper clips, staplers, pens, stickers, and other office supplies were listed. Hazel ordered business cards for herself and the other management people with the Center's logo on them, so they all were consistent.

Next, she drove to a discount store to pick up small towels and a new water bottle. She wanted to get permission to order special towels and water bottles with the Sports Center logo on them, but she still had some research to do on it before she presented the idea to Ross and Mike.

As she headed back to Lilac Lake, satisfaction filled Hazel. She liked being in charge and organizing everything. She was nervous about her upcoming tennis lessons but wasn't going to let that stop her from doing her job. Besides, after being relatively inactive during the winter and spring months, she was eager to get back in shape.

Mike left for a quick business trip to Florida, giving Hazel time to practice hitting tennis balls on her own. She started a routine of getting up early to go to the Center to use one of the automatic tennis ball machines on one of the courts.

On the third morning of seeing the same boy sitting on the grass outside the fence watching her, Hazel's curiosity got the best of her. She walked over to him.

Up close, she could see he was about ten years old, with auburn hair and a sprinkle of freckles across his nose. He looked up at her with hazel eyes and stood, prepared to run.

"Hi," she said, smiling. "I'm Hazel. Who are you? I see you here in the mornings. Do you play tennis?"

He studied her, as if assessing her, and said, "I'm Jed. Jed Abbott. I'd like to play tennis, but my foster mom says we can't afford it."

"Have you ever played?" she asked, drawn to the longing

in his face.

"Yes. I went to a day camp in my other foster home. The tennis teacher told me I was really good."

Hazel's heart went out to the little boy. She couldn't imagine what his life was like, going from one foster home to the next.

"Come around to the gate," said Hazel. "I'll lend my racket to you. Let's see what you can do."

Grinning, Jed sprinted to the gate and entered the court.

Hazel noticed he was wearing sneakers, a pair of jeans that were a little short on him, and a navy shirt with no design.

She saw that the size of his hand was almost as big as hers and could hold the racket easily. "Here. You take this and show me the grip you use."

Eyes alight with excitement, he held the racket out to show her.

Hazel had him move his hand a bit and said, "Okay, stand on the other side of the net and I'll toss some balls to you. You remember how to stand properly to hit the ball, don't you?"

"Yes." He trotted to the far side of the opposite court.

She threw a ball in his direction and watched as he rushed forward, easily swinging the racket and hitting the ball.

The ball was out, but it didn't matter; Jed's form was perfect.

Hazel tossed several more balls to Jed. Each time, the ball was returned. Not always in, and sometimes hitting the net, but his eye-hand coordination was phenomenal.

After a while, Hazel said, "We'd better pick up the balls. The Center will open shortly. But, Jed, meet me here tomorrow and every morning this week. And when the tennis pro returns next week, we'll show him together what you can do. In the meantime, you playing here will be our secret. Okay?"

Jed moved his head up and down enthusiastically.

Hazel hurried home to change for work, but her mind stayed on the adorable boy who was extremely talented. She hoped Mike wouldn't be upset with her, but she wanted to give Jed the chance to play at the Center, even if the cost came from her salary.

For the next several mornings, Hazel met Jed for some private practice. Each time Hazel saw Jed play, she knew she was right. He was no ordinary player.

After meeting Jed in the mornings, Hazel remained busy on the job. She was pleased to discover she liked making posters and announcements and seemed to have a knack for putting them together in colorful displays.

Tom and Ross met over the retail operation and came to a quick agreement. The office next to the reception desk would serve as the store's display of goods and equipment. Hazel developed purchase order sheets and instructed the reception staff on how to handle requests for orders. Evie Jeffries would make sure the displays were changed regularly.

Hazel ordered baseball hats, T-shirts, water bottles, and towels with the Center logo to be sold separately from the store's collection.

As Hazel and Ross discussed, the more advertising the Center could do, the better the chance of attracting new customers.

Hazel also looked into special rates at the Lilac Lake Inn,

and with Ross Roberts as a part-owner, an agreement was easily reached to offer discounts to Sports Center members and vice versa.

With Mike's absence, Tracy handled group lessons. Though Hazel wasn't included as an assistant, Tracy called on her to handle any paperwork associated with the class, including tracking who was present and who would attend the next class. Something Hazel had been told that Tracy would take care of. But Hazel didn't complain. She had other things on her mind.

CHAPTER SIX

ON **S**ATURDAY, **H**AZEL **WALKED INTO** **J**AKE'S, **EAGER TO** see her friends. She wasn't the only one who was busy during the summer. New Hampshire, a summer playground, came alive in those months, with tourists coming to the various lakes in the region. Lilac Lake drew its share of people, and with its charming town, the visitors' population grew.

Even now, Hazel was forced to wend her way carefully through the bar crowd to get to the table the locals had reserved.

As she emerged, she saw Mike and Tracy talking to friends. Smiling, she greeted them and then sat with Misty and Taylor, discussing Taylor's new book based on some of her New York experiences.

Aaron Collister and Sarah showed up.

Hazel was glad to see them, aware that with Sarah's parents back in town for the summer, Sarah had more free time away from working at the hardware store and caring for her twin daughters.

"Where's Whitney? And Nick?" Hazel asked the group.

"Nick is at work. As police chief, he finds the summer months super busy," said Taylor. "And Whitney is getting close to delivering their second baby. They haven't found out the sex yet, but Dani and I are praying it's a little girl to spoil."

Hazel was silent. Taylor wasn't trying for a baby, but Dani and Brad were. So far, no success.

Everyone ordered drinks and food, and it grew quiet as people dug into their meal.

Hazel treated herself to fish and chips and reminded herself that she'd need to work extra hard at tennis the next day. Thinking of Jed, Hazel waited until Tracy left to go to the restroom and then asked Mike to meet her tomorrow at the Center before it opened. "I have something to discuss with you privately."

"Okay," said Mike.

Craig Evans arrived, and Hazel introduced him to the others and encouraged him to sit beside her. She liked the fact that the local group continued to grow as more people her age took part in running the community.

When some people got up to leave, Hazel followed, suddenly realizing how exhausted she was.

The next morning, Hazel awoke and got ready for her tennis workout. She'd given Jed her old racket and packed her new one in its case, along with a canvas bag holding some things she'd need for work.

After she parked her car at the Center, she went around to the tennis courts and was pleased to see Jed waiting for her.

"' Morning," said Hazel. "Our tennis pro is back. I want him to meet you and to see how well you play."

"Okay," said Jed, looking up at Mike as he approached them.

"Hello," said Mike, studying the boy.

"This is Jed Abbott, who lives nearby in a foster home. He loves tennis and wants to play here. I've given him my racket and will pay for any of his classes," said Hazel.

Mike's look of surprise was quickly masked as he turned toward Jed.

"So, you're a foster kid. How did you learn to play tennis?" he asked Jed.

"At my other foster house, they sent me to camp. I learned there," said Jed proudly. "Hazel is helping me here. I'm good."

Mike chuckled. "Well, let's see you play. Run ahead and get ready on the court. I want to talk to Hazel for a minute."

Jed went through the gate and onto the court.

"So, this is the kid that Tracy complained to Ross about? She caught you one morning working with him and knew he didn't belong here," said Mike.

Hazel drew herself up. "Jed Abbott has as much right to be here as any other kid who can afford to play. I'm paying for him, so there should be no problem."

"I agree. Foster kid life is tough, and if we can help him, I see no reason not to."

"He's a phenom," said Hazel. "Anyone can see that." She was furious that Tracy had run to Ross about it without talking to her first.

"Let's see," said Mike.

They walked onto the near end of the court.

Mike picked up a ball and tossed it over the net.

"Wham!" The ball came roaring past his ear.

Mike glanced at Hazel and grinned. "Okay, Jed. I'll place the ball in different areas. Let's see how you do with them."

Ball after ball was tossed and returned.

Finally, Mike walked around the net to Jed and shook his hand. "You have more to learn, but you're a natural. If you don't mind, I'd like to talk to your foster parents about your playing tennis here."

"They'll tell you they can't afford for me to play," said Jed. "Hazel and I have been meeting in secret."

"Let me talk to them. Don't worry about the expense, we'll take care of it," said Mike. "I want to make sure they know and approve of your time here. I see you have a racket. We can get you some proper shoes and whatever else you need. Understand?"

Jed's eyes widened, and his jaw dropped. He darted to Hazel and hugged her.

Tears filled Hazel's eyes as she hugged him back. Looking up at Mike, she could see emotion on his face before he erased it.

"Let's go and meet with them now," Hazel said to Mike.

As Jed walked ahead of them, Mike said quietly to Hazel, "You've done a big kindness to him. I appreciate that."

"And I thank you for being so agreeable. Jed is a kid who needs a break, and we can give that to him."

Mike patted her on the back. "No worries. The Center will pick up the expense and call it a scholarship program."

"Thanks," said Hazel, stepping onto the front porch of a nearby house with Jed.

Mike rang the bell.

A heavy-set woman who looked to be in her forties came to the door carrying a baby and holding onto a toddler at her side. "Yes, what is it? Is Jed in trouble?"

"Not at all," said Mike. He introduced Hazel and himself and explained what they wanted to do.

"Why, that's the nicest thing I've heard in a long time,"

said the woman who introduced herself as Lisa Hunt. "My husband and I can barely make ends meet. As much as we might like to, we can't afford things like tennis lessons, even for an outstanding kid like Jed." She nudged Jed. "What do you say for yourself?"

Jed shuffled his feet. "Thank you, Hazel. Thank you, Mike."

"Well, now," said Lisa. "We can work around the time that Jed comes to the Center. Other times, he needs to help me out. I have a special-needs child inside."

"How old is the child?" Hazel asked, thinking Lisa already had her hands full.

"Lucinda is four, though she's a few years behind developmentally. Jed, here, is sweet about helping her exercise. We're hoping she'll walk soon."

"She will. I just know it," said Jed, and Hazel wanted to hug him. He was such a sweet boy.

"Why don't we continue to have Jed come to the Center at the same time as he has been doing?" said Lisa.

"And if we want him to come to a group lesson to meet other kids, we'll clear it with you," said Mike. "Does that sound like an acceptable plan?"

"Yes," said Lisa. "My husband works nights and tries to sleep during the day. He'll step in and help when Jed is out of the house."

"Thank you so much," said Hazel, touched by Lisa's willingness to work things out so Jed could play. "We have every reason to think that Jed is an exceptional player. And if this will give him opportunities in the future, that would be a blessing."

"Indeed," said Lisa, smiling at Jed. "You're a good boy. You deserve this."

Jed's cheeks grew red, and his eyes filled, but a look of determination kept those tears from leaking.

"See you tomorrow, Jed," said Hazel. "I'll have some shoes and tennis clothes for you to try on."

"Okay," he responded.

"See you," said Mike. "And thanks again, Lisa."

Hazel and Mike left the house and headed toward the Sports Center.

When they were far enough away, Hazel stopped and wiped tears from her cheeks. Mike put an arm around her.

"It's so sad," said Hazel. "I wish we could do more for that family. Poor Lisa has her hands full, and she still shows kindness."

"It isn't always that way," said Mike with such certainty that Hazel looked up at him.

Mike's eyes were shiny and his mouth was set.

"Oh, my God! Were you a foster kid?" she asked.

He nodded and walked away, staring down at the sidewalk.

Hazel hurried to catch up to him. "I'm sorry. This must be so hard for you."

Mike shrugged. "It makes me feel good to know there are some decent people out there. I just didn't know many until I got a break by playing tennis, just like Jed."

"I'll continue practicing with him in the morning before work, and then maybe you can give him lessons," said Hazel. "I can only give him a chance to practice."

"I owe you some tennis lessons. We can do some evening

lessons if that's okay with you. It should be cooler by then."

"It sounds great," said Hazel. "I need to brush up on my game."

He gave her a surprisingly shy glance. "It'll give us a chance to practice convincing your family we're together."

"I'm very embarrassed about that," said Hazel. "Hopefully, my family will stay away."

CHAPTER SEVEN

Hazel returned to the Center with a list of things she wanted to buy for Jed. She decided to drive to Concord to pick out those items at Access Sports. This would allow her to consider what they might display at the Center for kids.

She checked in with Ross, who was in his office, and told him what she had in mind.

"I understand you've been helping this boy on your own," said Ross. "Thank you. We need to encourage kindness and give everyone a chance at whatever sport they choose."

"Yes," said Hazel. She hesitated and then said, "I had no idea that Mike was a foster kid."

Appearing solemn, Ross said, "It wasn't an easy childhood. He doesn't usually talk about it."

"Helping Jed might be helpful to him," said Hazel. "The family Jed is with are caring people. I don't know how his foster mother does it. Four kids in the house, one disabled."

"Keep me informed of any way we can help them," said Ross. "I like that Jed will be part of a new scholarship program. Mike and I are very lucky to have hired you, Hazel."

After Nolan Deere's disapproval, Ross's words touched her. She gave him a little wave and left to go to Concord.

On the way, she thought about the situation with Jed and wondered how he'd fare with the other kids in tennis camp. Kids who came from homes that could afford it.

#

Hazel met with Evie as planned, and after explaining what she was trying to do for Jed, she and Evie walked through the store.

"Such beautiful things for kids. But surely, they outgrow them. What about setting up a second-hand department for them?" asked Hazel. "Or we could have customers turn in outgrown clothing to the Center so we could give them away or sell them for next to nothing."

"Yes! For those who turn in clothes that are in excellent shape, we can give them a discount to buy new clothes," said Evie. She clapped her hands together. "I'm so glad we're willing to work together. It's not just good business, it's just plain goodness."

The women smiled at one another.

"I've sized up clothing and shoes for Jed in my mind, so I'd like to get a couple of choices, in case I need a different size. I'll bring back the things we can't use. Or better yet, come to the Center and I'll treat you to lunch at the Lilac Lake Café," said Hazel.

"I'd love that," said Evie. "Let's pick out some things for Jed, and you can let me know when you want to meet. I'm pretty flexible with store hours, so I can arrange to get together anytime."

Hazel had seen Jed only in jeans and wearing old basketball shoes, but with Evie's help, she could select several choices of shoes and clothes in a couple of different sizes. She also needed to think of styles that would be comfortable on and off the court.

When she was satisfied with their selection, Hazel bid

Evie goodbye and drove to Office Depot for more office supplies, grateful for Mike and Ross's support in making decisions about things like this.

That afternoon, Hazel walked over to the tennis court where Mike was giving a private lesson to Jed. Hazel could assess both of them sitting on a bench outside the fence.

Watching Mike play tennis was like watching a ballet dancer move around the court with one graceful move after another at high speed. Even the way Mike swung his racket was done smoothly and so quickly that it seemed part of a performance.

Tracy joined her on the bench. "He's a star, huh?"

Hazel nodded and turned back to the training game. "Jed is really something. Mike is so patient with him."

Mike noticed them and called Tracy. "Come here and play with Jed so I can study his moves."

Sighing noisily, Tracy grabbed her tennis racket and went onto the court.

Mike came and sat beside Hazel. "Okay Tracy, play an easy, slow game so I can take notes on Jed's movements."

Hazel kept quiet as Mike studied the game on the court. After several minutes, he stood and called Jed over to him. "Tomorrow, when you practice with Hazel, you will work on your backhand. Remember what I told you."

Jed said, "I will."

Hazel stood. "Jed, I have some things I want you to try on. Please come to my office when you're through here."

"Okay," Jed said, his eyes lighting with excitement.

In her office, Hazel lined up shorts, shirts, socks, and

shoes for Jed. Seeing them like this, satisfaction filled her. The Sports Center required tennis wear on the courts, and she didn't want him to feel left out or unable to compete with the other kids socially.

When Jed walked into her office and saw the clothing laid out on her desk, he grinned.

"I've got different sizes for each item so we can make sure they fit you properly," said Hazel.

"They're all new," Jed said, and Hazel realized he wasn't used to that.

"Let's see." She held up various shorts for him to try on and quickly decided on the T-shirt size for him.

"Go ahead and try the shorts on in the men's room and come show me. I'll be standing outside the door. We want to narrow it down to one in white and another in black."

Hazel followed him to the men's room and waited for Jed to appear.

Grinning, Jed modeled three different pairs of shorts on him, and they quickly selected two. Then they chose four T-shirts with varying sayings of tennis and logos, plus two Sports Center shirts.

"Now for the sneakers. Here are some socks. Try this pair. They look about right for you."

Jed sat in a chair and slipped on the sneakers, tying them carefully.

Hazel checked for room in the toe. "This one will do."

"These are all for me?" asked Jed.

"Yes. If you're going to be part of the tennis program here at the Center, you need the right clothing and equipment." She handed him a small canvas bag. "Inside are some towels, a visor, a cap, and a water bottle. Oh, and a can of tennis balls, even though we will provide them for the classes."

"This is like the best Christmas I ever had," said Jed, beaming at her. "Thank you."

"You're welcome. It's wonderful to have you be a part of the Center. You're a really good player, Jed. We'll help you any way we can."

"I'll practice every day," Jed said solemnly, and at the gratitude she heard in his voice. Hazel felt a sting of tears.

Mike knocked on the door and entered. "Is our young champion ready now?" He glanced at the clothes and shoes. "It looks that way. Thank you, Hazel, for taking care of this."

"You're welcome," Hazel said. "It makes a big difference."

Mike studied her and grinned.

Tracy stopped in. "There you are, Mike. I'm done for the day, and you promised me a dinner if I'd take one of your classes."

He checked his watch. "Let's say eight o'clock. I still have to give Hazel a lesson and then I'll get ready. One of the staff will close up the tennis courts for me at dusk."

Tracy's lips formed a pout. "Well, you'd better not be late." She glanced at Hazel. "Make sure he's on time."

Hazel bobbed her head but remained quiet. She didn't want to get in the middle of any disagreements between those two.

After Tracy left, Mike said to Jed. "Do you want me to help you carry those things home?

Jed shook his head firmly. "No, I can get them." He held up the plastic bag with his sneakers and clothing, and lifted the canvas bag.

He stopped at the doorway and turned to them. "Thanks."

"The kid has gotta be overjoyed," said Mike after Jed had walked away. "That's like Christmas for him."

Hazel gave him a wide smile. "That's exactly what he said. I'm delighted we could do this."

Mike studied her. "I used to think you were a spoiled Southern Belle. Now, I know you're not."

"We went on only one date," said Hazel. "I know you better now, too."

"Let's get that tennis lesson in before I have to leave," said Mike, glancing at his watch.

"Okay, I'll meet you on the court in five minutes. I need to change," said Hazel.

When Hazel stepped onto the court, she noticed Mike's look of approval and was pleased she'd been able to buy a couple of tennis outfits for herself. She was normally healthy and in good shape, or so she'd thought, but activity here at the Center had her using muscles her body had forgotten.

Mike and she started volleying back and forth to warm up.

Though Hazel was very aware of Mike watching her every move, she thought she was holding her own until Mike stopped and waved her toward the net.

"I notice that your timing is just a bit off. Try moving more quickly in anticipation of the stroke of your arm so that you have better control. Especially with your backhand."

"Okay," said Hazel. "I want to be the best I can be. We're forming a tennis league for women, and I want to be at least able to keep up with the best of them. We have some really good players."

"You certainly can help with beginners. Especially with young children. Ross and I thought you'd fill that role perfectly."

"I'll try my best," said Hazel, realizing she needed to fine-tune her schedule. Now that the administrative job was under better control, she could be a help in other ways. She knew Ross and Mike had hired more staff and would continue to do so as their activities grew. Several people were required to oversee activities just to cover the hours of operation.

After hitting a few more balls, Hazel stopped. "Can we work on my serve?"

"Sure," said Mike. "Let's see what you've got."

Hazel moved a basket of balls over to the baseline where she stood and started serving.

Mike came around the net and watched her from the side.

After struggling, Hazel finally hit a few good ones. "I guess I need more practice."

"Yes. We'll work on that another time. Take a break."

He sat down on an outside bench, and Hazel joined him.

"Where did you learn to play tennis?" Mike asked her before taking a sip of water.

Hazel hesitated, then gave him a sly smile. "At the country club, like a spoiled Southern Belle."

He laughed, almost choking on the water. "Sorry about that."

Hazel checked her watch. "I guess we'd better get moving. You don't want to be late for dinner, and I know you have other things to do."

Mike frowned, but he got to his feet. "Okay, let me know when you're ready to work on your serve. Maybe I'll stop by some morning when I know you're at the courts."

"Okay," said Hazel. They walked back to the facility, and Hazel went to her office. It felt comforting to know that she and Mike didn't dislike one another anymore. Maybe they could get away with fooling her family if her mom visited as she'd mentioned.

CHAPTER EIGHT

WHEN TAYLOR CALLED TO INVITE HAZEL TO A GIRLS' DAY of relaxation at the Lilac Lake Cottage, Hazel was delighted to have some downtime. She'd been working hard and staying late at the office. With no scheduled meetings, she quickly accepted and followed up with a note to Mike and Ross that she would take the day off after seeing everything was okay.

That morning was what some New Englanders would call a "high sparkler," with bright-blue skies and plenty of sunshine spreading warmth and light. For once, Hazel allowed herself to stay in bed after the alarm went off. She loved moments like these, where she could lie quietly and sort through thoughts and ideas.

After she dressed for the day in her swimsuit, Hazel packed a towel, sunscreen, and a change of clothes in a canvas bag. Then she pulled together some food items. She'd promised to bring a coffee cake from the Lilac Lake Café, a bottle of wine for later, and some munchies. The Gilford sisters were generous about opening their cottage for parties, but everyone else provided most of the food for those events. Today was no different.

Because so many people were working, the party was limited to the three Gilford women, Misty, Crystal, Melissa, and her. A few other women promised to come after work. Hazel was excited to be able to spend some time with these women. It would give her a better idea of what it must have been like being together during their growing-up years.

When she arrived, she saw that the six other women were dressed in bathing suits with cover-ups, as well.

Taylor greeted her with a hug. "So glad you could make it, Hazel. I know how busy you are with the Sports Center."

"I've needed this break. Thank you so much for inviting me."

A group of women chatted in the kitchen. When they saw the coffee cake Taylor had brought, they eagerly waited for her to cut and distribute pieces of it.

Whitney, who was due to have her second baby any day, turned to Hazel. "I heard you're setting up a babysitting service at the Sports Center for mothers who want to play tennis and pickleball. That's fantastic. So many positive changes are taking place there since you became Administrator."

"I hope so," said Hazel. "I did a lot of research as to what other clubs and gyms were providing their customers."

"Ross admitted to me that programming and running the Center needed a woman's touch," said Melissa. "He's used to working with men. Now, he's even talking about having the girls' high school softball team come in for practice and pointers."

"It's wonderful for the community to have the Center. Ross and Mike should be proud of themselves for pursuing that idea," said Taylor.

"Okay, ladies, we have had the coffee cake from the Café," said Melissa. "Now I want you to taste test a recipe I've created for my cookbook. Please let me know both the good and the bad aspects of its taste, texture, and overall appearance. It's easy to make, so I have that factor covered."

Hazel helped herself to a piece of the apricot crumble cake that Melissa served on individual plates. Hazel was an adequate cook, but that was all. Growing up, her family had a housekeeper who cooked, and Hazel was never excited to be in the kitchen.

"Well?" asked Melissa after everyone in the group had taken a taste and more. She held a notebook in her hand.

As they all gave their responses, Melissa wrote them down. "Okay, it seems like everyone loved the flavor but wanted it to be a bit moister. I can take care of that. Thank you, ladies."

"It's such a beautiful day, let's take our coffee down to the rock," said Dani.

At the lake's edge, a huge granite rock rose out of the water. Its large, almost flat surface provided plenty of space for sunbathing and conversation.

"If I sit on the rock, at least two of you will have to help me up," said Whitney, rubbing her belly. "Carrying this baby, I'm so out of balance that it's almost impossible for me to move normally."

"We'll bring a chair," said Crystal. "It might be easier for you."

The women grabbed water bottles, towels, and sunscreen and headed down the sloped green lawn to the rock, with Crystal carrying a chair and Dani helping Whitney.

"We used to spend hours on this rock during the summers," Misty explained to Hazel. "Growing up in Lilac Lake was a great place for a kid."

"It's nice that y'all are still friends," said Hazel, gazing at the group. She had friends at home, but lately, their life choices were pulling them apart. Not that Hazel would change her mind about going back to Louisiana.

With their towels spread on the rock and Whitney settled in her beach chair, the women grew quiet as they lay, eyes closed, faces toward the sun.

Whitney broke the silence. "Uh-oh. Wait. Oh, my God! My water just broke."

Crystal, who assisted her husband at the Emergency Center, was the first to get to her. "Yes, I see. Okay, Whitney, we'll get you to the hospital."

"Timothy came quickly, and I think this baby is going to do the same thing," said Whitney, letting out a long groan.

"What'll we do?" asked Taylor.

"Let's get you to the Emergency Center. You can have your baby there," said Crystal, speaking calmly. "Hazel, you and Misty better walk Whitney up the hill. Dani, we'll take her in your truck. It has more room than some of our other vehicles. I'm calling Emmett now."

While Crystal sprinted up the hill to the cottage, Hazel took hold of one of Whitney's arms, and Misty, the other.

Halfway up the hill, Whitney stopped, clutched her stomach, and let out a long, low growl. "Oh, God! I've had what I thought were Braxton Hick's pains. I should have known this little one would be too impatient to wait."

Walking beside Hazel, Melissa said, "I'm calling Nick now. Is he home with Timothy?"

"Nick's at work. GG is with Tim while he has his morning nap."

When Melissa called, Nick's private line was busy. "Crystal must be talking to him. We'll check with her when we get to Dani's truck."

Whitney stopped by the truck and, clutching Hazel's fingers, let out another groan.

Feeling as if her hand was crushed, Hazel crooned, "It's going to be fine." She hoped she was right. She'd never been part of childbirth like this.

"Emmett's ready for you, and I've spoken to Nick," said Crystal as they approached her. She'd spread a clean towel on the back seat of Dani's truck. "Let's get you inside."

In minutes, Whitney was settled in the back seat, and Dani started the engine.

"I'll ride with Dani and Whitney," said Crystal to the other women. "We'll meet you there."

"C'mon, you can ride in my car," said Melissa. "I don't want to miss this."

Hazel, Misty, and Taylor climbed into Melissa's SUV, and they followed Dani's truck to the Emergency Center.

Nick's police car was already in the parking lot when they pulled in.

After Melissa parked, Hazel and the others climbed out of the car and went inside the reception area to wait.

Crystal joined them. "Emmett, Nick, and a nurse are with Whitney. Emmett said it's a good thing we brought Whitney here to the Clinic. It won't be long."

"I've never been this close to a birth before," said Hazel. "I thought babies took a long time to come."

"They usually do," said Crystal. "Second babies often come faster. In this case, that's certainly happening."

"I don't believe they know the sex of the child," said Melissa. "Whitney told me they wanted it to be a surprise."

"In the end, it doesn't matter, does it? As long as the baby is healthy," said Dani with a wistfulness they all understood. It was well-known in the group that Dani and Brad had been trying for a baby for several months.

Hazel, like the other women, settled down to wait. She didn't want to lose out on the excitement of finding out the sex of the baby. Though some of the women were married and others were engaged, Whitney was the first of their small group to have children. Others in their larger circle of friends, like Beth Beckman, already had a child.

Still in their bathing suits, the group grew quiet, giving Hazel time to think about her life. She'd pushed back on her mother's idea of when and who she should marry, but that didn't mean that she didn't want to have a man in her life. And even though seeing Whitney in such pain was a bit scary, she'd always wanted children.

Hazel was playing a game on her cell phone when Nick entered the waiting room. "It's a girl! Whitney wants you all to see the baby. They're both getting cleaned up. I'll let you know when they're ready."

He disappeared, and Hazel was as excited as the other women.

"I think we should all make this little girl a special member of our group," said Misty.

"Yes, of course," said Dani.

"We can all be aunties to her," Taylor said graciously.

Hazel and the others smiled at one another. It was the perfect Lilac Lake thing to do.

#

When Nick came to get them, the women were more than eager to follow him into a private exam room, which had been turned into a birthing room for Whitney.

"Hi, everyone. I want you to meet Lily Eugenia Gilford Woodruff. Isn't she beautiful?"

Whitney held a red-faced newborn who let out a lusty cry.

"GG will be thrilled you've given Lily her middle name," said Taylor.

"That's so adorable," said Dani.

"We've decided that we'll all be aunties to Lily," said Crystal. "She'll always be loved and protected and spoiled by us."

Whitney's face crumpled and tears escaped her eyes. "That's the sweetest thing ever."

Emmett walked into the room and stood by Nick. "Okay, everyone, mother and daughter need a little time to themselves."

The women left, and as soon as they were outside, Taylor said, "Is everyone ready to return to the cottage? We have bubbly wine and lots of food for a celebration."

The six of them returned to the cottage, feeling even closer after they'd shared this experience today. Hazel felt privileged to be part of such a giving group. This was just one reason Hazel didn't want to leave town.

CHAPTER NINE

THE NEXT MORNING, A LITTLE SUNBURNED, HAZEL returned to the Sports Center for her early practice with Jed. It touched her that Jed was never late for his special time with her.

When she walked onto the court, she was confused by seeing Mike there.

"Hope you don't mind. I thought this might be an agreeable time for both of you to work on your serves."

"That's fine with me," said Hazel, hoping the wine and sun of yesterday wouldn't affect her performance. It had been such a crazy, fun celebration.

"Line up at the baseline, one on each side," said Mike. "I'll watch you. And even though we're concentrating on serving, if a ball comes over the net, the receiver should try to hit it back. Hazel, we're starting with you."

Hazel got into position, tossed the ball in the air, and hit it into the net.

"Okay. This is for both of you. How you toss the ball is very important. If you toss it too far forward, you'll have to reach to hit it, swinging too late to place the ball where you want it over the net."

For the next hour, Hazel and Jed practiced their serves. Hazel wasn't the least bit intimidated when she realized she and Jed played equally well. She knew he'd soon move on to playing with someone better. Someone like Mike.

When Mike called an end to the practice, Hazel sat on the

bench outside the court, mopping her face with her towel and sipping the water she'd brought.

Jed and Mike did the same.

They were sitting together, talking, and laughing when Tracy appeared.

"What's going on?" she asked, frowning.

"We've just completed a lesson," said Mike.

Tracy put her hands on her hips and stared at him. "So that's where you went? When I woke up, you were gone."

"I told you I had a lesson this morning," said Mike evenly.

"Well, I didn't know it was with Hazel and this boy," Tracy responded with an annoying edge to her voice.

Jed gazed at Hazel. She decided not to speak, figuring no matter what she said, it would be misinterpreted.

Mike got to his feet. "Thanks, guys, we'll do this again. And, Jed, remember to come to the camp tournament this afternoon. Here's a note to take to your foster mom."

"Thanks," said Jed. "Guess I'd better go home. See you tomorrow, Hazel."

"Sure thing," Hazel said, rising. She had to take a shower and change out of her clothes before her workday started.

Later, she was brushing her hair in the women's locker room when Tracy approached her.

"Hey, thought we'd better talk," said Tracy. "I'm serious about Mike and me being together. I don't want you interfering with that."

Hazel gave her a steady look. "Mike and I have an understanding. We're not interested in any relationship beyond friendship. He's my boss. It's always a bad idea to have a work relationship become more than that."

"Okay, just so we're both in agreement," said Tracy. "He's someone impressive in the tennis world, and that's important to me. I know you come from a different background, but I've worked very hard to get where I am, and I'll do what I must to get ahead."

"I admire ambition. I do," said Hazel. "But you may have the wrong idea about me."

Tracy's gaze swept up Hazel's body and back down again. "Maybe not."

Hazel sighed as Tracy strode away. She prayed her family would stay away from Lilac Lake. It would only cause more friction at work.

That evening, as Hazel was doing laundry, her cell phone rang. *Her mother.*

Hazel groaned and picked up the call. "Hi, Mom! What's up? How's your country club dance coming along?"

"It's coming together," said her mother. "I wish you'd come home for it. I found the loveliest dress for you to wear. It's going to be the social event of the summer."

"It's sweet of you to think of me," Hazel said, hoping she sounded truthful. "But you know I can't leave."

"I thought you'd say that, which is why Elliott is coming north to visit you. He's quit his job at the bank, and while he has some free time, his mother and I thought a visit to Lilac Lake might be in order. That will give you both time to think."

"Mom, you know nothing will change," said Hazel.

"It's helpful for you and Elliott to have some time together. What happens after that is up to the two of you."

"He's welcome to stay with me. I have a guest room he

can use," said Hazel. "I assume he's going to call me or is his mother going to do that for him?" It was such a difficult situation and had caused Elliott to keep secrets.

"I'll let Elliott's mother know you've agreed to it, but he must call you himself," said her mother.

"Agreed," said Hazel.

After chatting with her mother about her social life, Hazel ended the call more certain than ever that she didn't want to go back home.

She'd just curled up in bed with a book when her cell phone rang. *Elliott.*

She picked up the call. "Hi. I knew I'd be hearing from you. My mother said you quit your job at the bank. That must have been traumatic for your father. Wasn't it your grandfather who formed that bank?"

"Yes, don't remind me. I've heard all about it over and over again. But I can't live this lie any longer. I need time away to pull myself together and then be open with my parents, knowing it will break their hearts."

"Oh, Elliott. That sounds so awful."

"But it's true. You, more than anyone, know that."

"Yes, I do. We've been best friends since we were kids, but I couldn't stay in our town to satisfy our mothers. Wait until you see Lilac Lake. It's such a pretty, friendly place. You'll love it."

"You don't mind putting me up for a while?" Elliott asked.

"I have a guest room you can use," said Hazel. "Who knows? You might decide to stay here."

"I have no idea what I'm going to do moving forward," said Elliott. "I'll have to give my parents time to reconsider things at home."

"When are you arriving?" asked Hazel, thinking it would be pleasant to have his company.

"I'll be driving north, and I should be there within a week. I may make a stop or two along the way."

"Whenever you get here, your guest room will be ready for you," said Hazel. "I've missed you, but I'm very happy living in Lilac Lake."

"No boyfriends yet?" asked Elliott.

"I haven't found the right guy," said Hazel. "Right now, I'm too busy to think of it as I get my arms around the job at the Sports Center."

"Well, we both have plenty of time," said Elliott. "I'll be in touch as I travel north."

"Okay, see you soon," Hazel said, pleased that Elliott was finally making this change in his life.

The next morning, Hazel was surprised once more to see Mike show up as she and Jed practiced hitting balls back and forth.

"I thought I'd give you two a workout," he said. "I'll be hitting balls back to both of you. We'll make a game of it. You two against me."

Jed looked at Hazel and grinned.

"We'll be the ones giving you a workout," said Hazel. "Right, Jed?"

"Right," he said proudly.

Hazel loved how Mike had effortlessly made Jed feel part of a group.

The game started slowly, with Mike allowing Hazel and

Jed to get used to the speed of the ball returned to them.

Then the game began in earnest, with Hazel and Jed learning to play doubles, stepping in when necessary, giving a partner room to play.

When Jed and Hazel began placing balls to keep Mike running, they all laughed as he tried to keep up. "Okay. I've had an excellent workout, and the two of you are playing well together. We'll have to include you in some doubles in your age group. Hazel, you are part of our tennis team, aren't you?"

"Yes," said Hazel. "I joined the other day and will be playing for the Center in local tournaments and some of the individual contests in the club."

"Okay. And, Jed, I'm placing you on the club's beginner's team, but I don't expect you to stay there very long. We'll see. It's important for you not to feel pressured but to simply have fun."

"I have a lot of fun here," Jed said.

"Good. Tracy is coming. I have to go," said Mike. "Jed, I'll see you this afternoon. Hazel, you might want to come to the tennis team practice to watch him."

Hazel smiled at both of them. "I'll try."

She was glad to see how much Mike cared about Jed and realized he was identifying with Jed's experience of being a foster child.

Later, when Hazel saw Craig in his office, she decided to talk to him about Elliott.

She knocked on his door, and at his response, she came inside the office and sat in a chair in front of his desk. "I hope I'm not disturbing you, but I need to ask you for some guidance on a personal issue."

Craig gave her a look of concern. "How can I help?"

Hazel told him about Elliott and his upcoming visit to Lilac Lake. "He's one of my best friends. And though we'll never marry like his family wants, I care about him very much. He's coming here to prepare to tell his parents he's gay, and that's why we won't ever be a couple."

"And how do you want me to help?" asked Craig, taking off his glasses and giving her a steady look.

"You've said you're comfortable with who you are. Perhaps you can talk to him about your journey," said Hazel, hoping she wasn't being too intrusive. "Elliott has hidden so much about his inner self from others. He must be twisted into knots. There's only so much I can say."

"Why is his family so threatened by the idea that Elliott is gay?" asked Craig.

"It's all part of their image and family connections. His grandfather founded the bank Elliott has turned his back on. His father is an important man in town. And he's supposed to uphold the family name. He's Elliott Gladstone III."

"I get it. Forgive me, but I think it's a crock of shit," said Craig. "If Elliott feels like talking to me, I'll be happy to help. But don't push him to do this."

"Thanks so much," said Hazel, rising. "You'll see for yourself what a likable guy Elliott is."

"It sounds like he has a lot to work out for himself," said Craig. "Now that you're here, I want to talk to you about the retail sales operation."

Soon, Hazel was caught up in business and didn't have the time to think about Elliott's arrival.

CHAPTER TEN

Several days later, when Elliott pulled into Hazel's driveway and got out of the car to stretch, Hazel's breath caught. She'd forgotten how handsome he was with his blond hair and blue eyes, trim but muscular physique, and classic features.

"You're here!" she cried, rushing toward him.

He opened his arms, and she ran into them.

They hugged and swayed together for several minutes before Hazel pulled away and stared into his face. "You look exhausted. Come inside and sit on the deck with me to rest before you bring your things inside."

He followed her into the cabin and gazed around. "This is nice and cozy."

"Come out to the deck with me. The view is lovely."

They went through the kitchen and onto the wooden deck overlooking woods and beyond to the river. The call of a cardinal filled the air.

Elliott turned to her with a grin. "The real outdoors. I like it."

"I've grown to love it. What would you like? Water? Coffee? Beer?"

"A cold beer sounds fantastic," said Elliott, standing at the deck's rail. He sighed. "It feels soothing to simply stand right here."

"I'll be right back," said Hazel, glad she'd taken the rest of the day off. She could see how much Elliott had needed to get away. There were circles beneath his eyes, and even as he smiled, she could see the tension on his face.

Moments later, she returned to the deck and handed Elliott a cold bottle of beer.

She clicked her bottle against his and said, "Here's to best friends."

"Ah, Hazel, you truly are my best friend," he responded. "All these years. Thank you for allowing me to stay with you until I get my life squared away. It isn't like I haven't tried to talk to my parents, but they refuse to believe their only child isn't the person they think he is."

"You've done so much to please them. Baseball, football, and swim team at the club."

"Being gay doesn't mean you can't be a sports professional," said Elliott. "But I've worked hard to give nothing away."

"There's someone I want you to meet. Craig Evans is the financial manager of the Sports Center and is a person you can talk to about your situation. But no rush. Give yourself time to relax and see why I like Lilac Lake so much."

"Sounds appealing. I need lots of rest."

"I thought we'd grill up some chicken for dinner and have a relaxing evening. I get up early to practice tennis with a ten-year-old boy I've taken under my wing. He's a foster kid who's adorable and very talented. Mike Dawson, the tennis pro at the Center, thinks he has a natural ability to do very well."

"That sounds like the Hazel I know," said Elliott. "Let's get my things inside. Your mother sent some of your favorite foods and treats. I've packed the frozen ones in a cooler."

"What a lovely surprise," said Hazel. There was no better food than that found in and around New Orleans. She loved it all.

They unloaded the car, and Hazel helped to store things out of the way in the large guestroom closet.

Elliott opened the window and breathed in the pine-scented air Hazel loved. "This is spectacular. I have a feeling I'm going to sleep like a baby."

"I promise not to wake you up in the morning," said Hazel. "Now, let's see what food my mother sent."

Hazel unloaded frozen containers of gumbo, crawfish etouffee, red beans and rice, a box of pralines, and even a box of well-packaged beignets.

"Let's skip the chicken. I'll make us some rice, and we can choose what New Orleans food we want for dinner," said Hazel.

"That sounds both delicious and easy," said Elliott, taking another bottle of beer out of the refrigerator. "One of these nights I'll make you some barbequed shrimp."

"I think I'm in heaven with all this delicious food," said Hazel, gazing at the packages of food he'd brought.

After dinner of rice and crawfish etouffee, Hazel quickly cleaned up. After seeing that Elliott was comfortable for the night, she went into her bedroom to read. She found reading was the best way for her to fall asleep, and she didn't want to be late in the morning.

Sometime in the night, she heard a noise coming from the guestroom and reminded herself it was just Elliott. Soon it was quiet, and when she opened her eyes, it was morning.

Quietly, Hazel got out of bed and dressed for tennis practice with Jed. The practices had become very important to her for several reasons. Her appearance meant that Jed could trust her to keep her word and her interest in him. Having Mike back that up from time to time with his presence was priceless.

When Hazel walked into the kitchen, she was surprised to see Elliott sitting at the table.

"You're up early," she said. "Couldn't sleep?"

"A couple of different kinds of birds were singing, and in the quiet, they woke me up. But it's all good. I'll relax around here today and take a couple of naps."

"If you feel up to it, we can have dinner at Jake's, the place where I hang out with my friends. It'll be an enjoyable way for you to meet some other people," said Hazel.

"Okay. Sounds good. You're off to tennis?"

"Yes, and then I'll go right into my office. While you're here, I'll try to take some time off so we can do some things together."

"Don't let me interfere. Your mother says you have a boyfriend here," said Elliott.

Hazel groaned and gave him a helpless look. "Not really. It's something that slipped out while I was trying to get her off my back about you."

He winked at her. "You can introduce him to me."

She laughed. " 'Oh, what a tangled web we weave, when first we practice to deceive.'"

"Oh, yes," he said, and Hazel caught bitterness in his tone of voice.

###

When Hazel rushed to the tennis court to meet Jed, he wasn't there. She checked her watch. Usually, he came a few minutes early, and today she was a little late.

Frowning, she took a seat on the bench to wait for him.

After fifteen minutes had gone by, Hazel tried Lisa's number, but Jed's foster mother didn't answer.

Hazel decided to go to the house to see why Jed hadn't come.

Concerned, she swiftly walked the block and a half to Lisa's house. Before she even climbed the front porch steps, she heard crying children.

Worried, she walked to the front door and rang the bell.

Jed answered the door carrying the youngest while a toddler followed behind.

"Hi, Jed. What's going on?" Hazel asked, seeing the frantic look on his face.

"Lisa is sick in bed. I need to stay here," Jed said.

"How about I help you? Would you like that?" asked Hazel.

He opened the screen door and let her inside. "I gave the baby a cookie and Harry some cereal, but I can't take care of Lucinda. I need you to help me."

Unsure what was needed, Hazel stepped inside.

The living room was a mess, with toys strewn about, an open cereal box on the coffee table, a half-full glass of juice nearby. In a crib in the corner, Lucinda lay on her back, staring up at her. It was obvious that she had a dirty diaper. The smell was awful.

Hazel gulped at the sight. "Jed, you need to show me

where to find new diapers and lotion for Lucinda. In the meantime, let's get Harry in his highchair and see if we can put the baby in his bouncer seat. First, I'll let Lisa know I'm here."

He nodded and placed the baby in his seat, and stood by as Hazel found her way to Lisa's bedroom.

She stopped at the doorway and peered inside. Lisa was lying in bed on her back.

"Hi, Lisa. Do you remember me? I'm Hazel from the Sports Center," she said, walking over to her. Lisa's face was flushed, and Hazel noticed beads of sweat on her forehead.

"Yes, I know you. I'm sick with some kind of flu. I'm burning up. My husband is coming home as soon as he can, but it won't be for a while."

"I'm going to help Jed see that the other children are fed and taken care of," said Hazel. "Lucinda needs to have her diaper changed. Tell me what to do with her."

"She's usually very compliant, but when you change her diaper, you need to sing to her to calm her. You can give her a bottle of special formula until I can get up and feed her more food myself. Jed knows I keep an emergency bottle for her in the refrigerator. Heat it until it's lukewarm."

"Harry. What does he get? Cereal and what else?" asked Hazel.

"I cut up some fruit for him or scramble an egg," said Lisa, her voice growing weaker. "The baby can get by with formula and some teething cookies."

Hazel noticed a bathroom nearby and went to it. She soaked a washcloth with cold water, wrung it out, and brought it to Lisa. "See if this feels better. Can I bring you a glass of water? Aspirin?"

"Yes, to both. Thanks. I've never been this sick. I'll get up in a while. In the meantime, please go ask my neighbor to come help. She's a nurse, and she and I have an arrangement to help out one another from time to time."

"Okay. If you need anything, please call out." Hazel took care of the water and aspirin, which she easily found in the bathroom, then backed out of the room and turned to face the disaster awaiting her.

"Okay, let's give the baby a bottle and Harry more cereal and some fruit," said Hazel. "Then I'm going to change Lucinda and give her a bottle."

Jed went to the refrigerator to get out two different bottles. "This one is for Lucinda." He pointed to one and ran the other bottle under warm water in the sink. "This is for Baby Simon."

"This is a lot of work for you," said Hazel, amazed at how calm and capable Jed was.

"Living with Lisa is a lot better than the other foster homes I had," said Jed. "Is Lisa going to be all right?"

"I think so. I need you to run to your neighbor's house and ask her to come."

Jed handed her the bottle for the baby and took off.

Hazel had just settled Baby Simon in his playpen eagerly sucking on his bottle, when a gray-haired, energetic woman followed Jed into the house.

"Hi. I'm Hazel Belmont, Jed's tennis teacher from the Sports Center. Are you the nurse?"

"Yes, I'm Janis Tolland." She tied the sash on her robe. "Jed tells me Lisa's sick."

"She's in bed with the flu. A moment ago, she was burning up. I've given her water and aspirin."

"Okay, let me check her, and then I can help you with Lucinda. She's used to me, and she can be a handful," said Janis.

Hazel felt a rush of relief. She'd always pictured herself with perfectly behaved, easy-going children one day. Seeing the reality of everyday life for Lisa, she knew she wasn't ready for them.

Still, Hazel went to work straightening the living room and then tackling the mess in the kitchen.

Harry spoke and offered her a Cheerio.

She pretended to take it and eat it, sending Harry into peals of laughter.

It became a game until they both tired of it.

Gazing at that sweet, brown-skinned boy, she reconsidered her thoughts about having children as long as it wasn't too soon.

Janis carried Lucinda into the kitchen. "Where's her bottle? Will you feed her?"

Hazel held up a bottle. "It's ready for her. Where do you want me to feed her?"

"On the couch in the living room. She likes to feel a part of the family," said Janis. "It looks like you have everything cleaned up. I'll check on Lisa. I'll leave to go home, but I'll be right back after I get dressed."

"Thank you. I'd appreciate that. I'm already late for work," said Hazel.

She went and sat on the couch and allowed Janis to lower Lucinda's body into her lap. Lucinda's dark eyes never left her face even as she took to the bottle that Hazel held for her.

Jed came and sat beside them.

Lucinda's eyes brightened at the sight of him.

He reached over and took hold of Lucinda's hand. "She's been eating some food lately. She's getting stronger every day on the shakes that Lisa makes for her."

Hazel nodded, too touched to respond. Jed was one of the sweetest people she'd ever met.

Janis came back and stood smiling at them. "Lucinda loves Jed."

"I can see why," said Hazel. "Did you know he's also a terrific tennis player? He's very talented, which is why the Sports Center is sponsoring him."

Janis smiled at Jed. "That's wonderful news, Jed. I'm proud of you."

"Thanks," said Jed shyly.

"I'll take over from here," Janis said to Hazel. "Thank you so much for your help. Lisa is such a dear woman, I'm glad to step in whenever I'm needed."

"She certainly works hard," said Hazel, allowing Janis to take Lucinda from her.

"An angel on earth," agreed Janis. "Jed, after Joe gets home, I'm sure you'll be able to join your tennis class."

He walked Hazel to the door.

"I hope to see you at the Center later," said Hazel. "If you need me for anything else, you can call. Okay?"

He nodded and gave her a thumbs-up.

Hazel walked back to the Center, hoping she wouldn't be called upon to help with any entitled kids. Not after being with Jed and his family.

###

When Hazel returned to the Sports Center, Tracy approached her. "Where were you? I needed you to help teach my beginners' class."

"I'm sorry. Jed's family had an emergency, and I was helping them out. I didn't think you'd mind. It's a small, early class," said Hazel as Mike approached.

"I heard you. Is everything all right with Jed and his family?" he asked Hazel.

"Lisa is sick, and things were in a bit of a mess. A neighbor is now helping out, but I had to lend a hand."

"She was supposed to be with me, teaching a class," said Tracy. "Not with our little tennis star's family."

Mike blinked and straightened. "Hazel was helping them, Tracy. You have no idea what Jed's family is like. If I were you, I'd back off."

"I give up," said Tracy. "No matter what I try to do to help you, it backfires. I'm not even sure l should stay."

"I'll see you two later," said Hazel. "I've got to go change." She didn't want any part in the argument brewing between the two of them.

Later, Mike approached her. "Thank you for caring about Jed and his family. It's kind of you."

"He's an exceptional kid. And when I see how hard Lisa works every day, I am in awe of her. The neighbor who came to help says she's a true angel."

Mike looked down at the ground. When he caught her gaze, there was a sadness in his eyes that touched her. "Many foster parents are like that. Unfortunately, some are not."

"I'm sorry you had some bad experiences," Hazel said. "You must be very proud of how well you've done to overcome them."

Mike studied her thoughtfully. "I'm off for a private lesson. See you later."

Hazel watched him go, thinking how much she admired him.

CHAPTER ELEVEN

AS SOON AS SHE COULD, **H**AZEL LEFT THE **C**ENTER TO GO home and check on Elliott. She hoped he hadn't been bored by being left on his own.

She arrived home to find him lounging on a deck chair reading a book.

"I was hoping you'd relax today. What are you reading?" she asked him, relieved to see him like this.

"A mystery. Something to take my mind off my problems. But now that you're here, I'm hoping you'll give me a tour of the town."

"No problem. I want you to see why I like it so much. We can get a late afternoon coffee at the Lilac Lake Café, and I'll show you Main Street. Tomorrow, I'll take you to a few of my favorite places out of town. And one day, we'll go to Portsmouth so you can see what that bit of history is about. Then, of course, we can get fresh lobster in Maine."

"Whoa!" said Elliott, laughing. "I'm not sure how long I'm staying."

"We'll do as much as we can in the time you're here," said Hazel, eager for him to understand her choices.

Later, after walking up and down Main Street, they sat on the patio of the Café drinking coffee and watching people stroll by.

"It's a busy place," said Elliott. "I can understand why. The downtown area is attractive with lots to offer. It's a slice of Americana, with the white-steepled churches, the high-end stores, the American flag on each lamp post, and pots of flowers everywhere."

"Yes, sometimes I think a picture of downtown should be on postcards mailed for everyone to see. But I, like the natives, don't want the town to change too much," said Hazel. She saw Taylor and waved her over.

"Taylor, I want you to meet my friend, Elliott Gladstone, who is here visiting me for a while. Elliott, this is Taylor Gilford Walker. She writes books under the name of Courtney Castle."

"Hello. I'm pleased to meet you," said Elliott in a southern drawl.

Taylor grinned. "You're from the south, too? We sometimes tease Hazel about her accent, but we all think it's charming."

Elliott laughed. "It's a little hard to get rid of, but I try."

"See? It's adorable," said Taylor, chuckling. "Are the two of you going to be at Jake's tonight?"

Elliott looked at Hazel.

"Yes, we're planning on it."

"See you later," said Taylor. "I promised Whitney I'd take some coffee and a piece of cake to her. The baby has been sleeping during the day and crying at night, and she's exhausted."

Hazel turned to Elliott. "My friends and I were practically witnesses to the birth, so we all feel especially close to this little one. A girl named Lily. Her middle name is Eugenia after her great-grandmother Eugenia Wittner, who is sort of like the matriarch of this town. Her family owned The Lilac Lake Inn until she sold it a few years ago."

"I guess in a small town everyone knows everyone's business," said Elliott.

"Yes, they do," Hazel said.

Elliott took a sip of coffee and set down his cup. "I appreciate being here, Hazel. I'd marry you in a heartbeat if I could. I know I've put pressure on you, too, by not speaking up. Why haven't you told your parents about me?"

Hazel gave him a steady look. "I wasn't kidding when I called you my friend. You're my best friend. I've always known you were gay, even as a teenager. But it's not my news to share. I haven't let it define our relationship. We come from similar backgrounds and have needed one another. Time and choices haven't changed that."

"Both sets of parents are old-fashioned. My father, especially," said Elliott. "I've already disappointed him by not being the sports star he was. That's one reason I've held off on coming out to him. I can't imagine how he'll feel about me then. Grandfather, too. When you're Elliott Gladstone III, it carries a lot of responsibility. Something I don't want."

"I know your parents," said Hazel. "It's going to be rough, but your parents will still love you underneath all the social standing concerns."

"I hope you're right," said Elliott. "Because I have to be true to myself."

"Agreed," Hazel said. "Remember, I have someone I want you to talk to. Hopefully, he'll be at Jake's tonight."

"Don't tell me he's gay," said Elliott.

"Actually, he is," said Hazel. "But he's comfortable with it. He might be a reliable resource. That's all I mean by it."

"Sorry. I don't mean to be difficult. I'm here for a reason, so any help you can give me will be appreciated. It seems ridiculous that someone in his late twenties should be so unsure."

"Not everyone has the pressure you've had for all of your life," said Hazel. "Let's walk back home. I want to show you a special park a friend of mine created in memory of his sister."

They strolled a couple of blocks from Main Street to a small garden bordered with colorful summer flowers on a pretty lot that held several benches placed strategically for comfort and privacy.

"You'll meet David Graham tonight at Jake's, I'm sure. He's engaged to a friend of mine, Misty Owens. He and his family designed and keep this garden park maintained. I love coming here when I want some time to think things over," said Hazel.

"It's really beautiful," said Elliott. He walked to the back corner and took a seat on the bench.

Hazel joined him and sat quietly listening to the sounds of bees hovering at flowers and birds chirping in the tree above them. It was a taste of nature at its best.

"I can see why you love this town so much," said Elliott. "I might decide to stay awhile." He glanced at her and chuckled. "I don't mean at your place. Maybe find a place of my own."

"I want you to stay with me as long as you want or need to," Hazel said graciously. "Let's be on our way."

When they entered the driveway leading to the group of cabins along the river, Poppy Browning drove up beside them and stopped her car. "Hi, Hazel. Are you coming to Jake's tonight?"

"Yes. I'm bringing my friend. This is Elliott Gladstone."

"Nice to meet you, Elliott. See you then," said Poppy, smiling at them both before pulling away.

"Poppy Browning is a fairly new neighbor of mine. A very sweet woman who owns The Wild Flower Boutique downtown," explained Hazel. "She and Blake Loomis are together. I have a feeling she'll end up moving back into the family home she sold him."

"Wow! Everyone seems to be connected to everyone else. What about you, Hazel? You've lied to your mother about the tennis pro. Is there anyone you're really interested in?"

"No. I want to keep my life simple. New people are moving to town all the time. I figure I'll know when I'm ready for someone who interests me," said Hazel. "I'm not in any rush. I like my new job. It keeps me challenged."

"You're a good friend and a very special person. I need to make sure you end up with someone worthy of you," said Elliott, putting a protective arm around her.

Hazel laughed. She and Elliott did love one another.

Hazel waited at the door for Elliott before taking off for Jake's.

He moved toward her, movie-star handsome in blue jeans and a black T-shirt that set off his shiny blond hair, worn brushed back.

"Ready? Even though it's a short distance, I'll drive. It

might make it easier later." She was excited for Elliott to meet her friends.

A short while later, when they walked into Jake's, all eyes turned to them. Hazel knew they weren't looking at her and kept walking to the back tables where the locals hung out.

Dani and Brad, Taylor and Cooper, Melissa and Ross, and Mike and Tracy were already there.

Hazel and Elliott sat down, and Hazel quickly introduced Elliott and then each person introduced themself.

When it came to Tracy, she beamed at him. "I'd love to show you around."

It seemed such an obvious move that Hazel wasn't the only one amused by it, and the way she was fluttering her fake eyelashes at him.

Poppy, Blake, and Craig appeared along with others, and the two tables became full of conversation as people chatted, ordered drinks and food, and caught up on local news.

Ross, sitting next to Hazel, wanted to talk about the tennis camp for beginners, and Hazel ignored what else was going on until Mike got up to leave.

"See everyone later," he said. "And, Hazel, I'll see you tomorrow morning for our practice session with Jed."

Tracy remained in her chair, arms crossed in front of her, a furious look on her face. "I'm staying."

Mike waved to the crowd and walked away.

"I'll drop you off on my way home," Craig said to Tracy.

"Thanks. Mike knows I'm not ready to go home. He's such a party pooper." She turned to Elliott. "But this will give me more of a chance to get to know you better."

Elliott shrugged. "Not that much to tell."

Hazel knew he was uncomfortable. He and Craig had exchanged friendly words but hadn't had a real chance to talk. Hopefully, that would change.

Elliott caught her eye, and she understood his silent message. "Elliott and I are going to head out. It was great to see everyone."

Elliott held her chair, and Hazel got to her feet.

As they started to walk away, Hazel heard Tracy say, "What a bummer of a night."

The next morning, Hazel made her way out of the house for her early morning tennis practice. She was relieved when she got to the Sports Center and saw both Jed and Mike waiting for her.

"' Morning," she said cheerfully. "It's going to be a hot one, so this is a smart time to practice."

"Elliott doesn't mind?" asked Mike.

Hazel's eyes widened. "Oh, you think we're together? No, he's why I had to lie to my mother." She glanced at Jed and back to Mike. "After we're through here, I'll explain."

"Okay. Now, we'll rotate, two against one."

"Me first," said Jed, and Mike and Hazel chuckled. Jed was gaining a lot of self-confidence.

The practice was a successful one. As the three of them sat on a bench afterward, Hazel wiped the sweat off her face and sipped her water.

"How would you like to play mixed doubles with me tonight?" Mike asked her.

"Don't you usually play with Tracy?" she asked.

"It wouldn't be fair to the other couple to have to play

against both Tracy and me. You and I would make a better team, and this will give me a chance to see how you play a real game of doubles."

"Okay," said Hazel. "I'd be honored to play with you. But after this, you might decide to choose a different partner."

"We'll see. I'll be tough on you," said Mike, grinning.

"I've got to go home," said Jed. "Thanks."

He left, and Mike turned to Hazel. "So, what's the deal with Elliott? And why does it include me?"

Hazel filled him in on the story. "So, he's going to stay with me for a while. I'm hoping he has a chance to talk to Craig."

"Craig's a good guy," said Mike. "Smart, too."

"What time is the doubles game tonight?" asked Hazel.

"Six o'clock. The group usually has drinks and snacks afterward. The other couple will provide them, so you don't need to worry about it."

"Who's playing us?" Hazel asked.

"I'm not sure. It's on a rotating schedule." He winked at her. "Check the new bulletin board."

She laughed. "Okay. I guess I'd better get to work."

She hoped Elliott wouldn't mind that she was playing tennis. But the opportunity to be on a team with Mike was too tempting to turn down. She just hoped she wouldn't embarrass them both.

CHAPTER TWELVE

THAT EVENING, HAZEL APPROACHED THE TENNIS COURT unusually nervous. Elliott hadn't been the least bit disappointed. Instead, he'd promised to meet Craig, and they'd both come to watch them play.

Mike was talking to a couple in their late forties. The brown-haired man with a bit of gray at his temples had a sturdy build. His wife was medium height and looked very fit in her tennis skirt and halter top.

When he noticed her, Mike waved her over. "Hazel, I want you to meet Ray and Libby Norris. They are faithful members of the Club in Florida and have recently joined the Sports Center here."

"Yes, I thought I recognized the name," said Hazel.

"We try to spend as much time up here during the summer when Florida is so hot," said Ray. "But I have businesses to run in Florida, so it's more of a transient thing."

Mike turned to Ray and Libby. "Hazel is the new administrator at the Center, which is why everything is so well organized with many new programs. Ross and I are grateful she's agreed to work for us."

"We visited the Center last summer and are very impressed with all the changes," said Libby, pushing her sunglasses atop her head and shaking Hazel's hand.

"In addition to her job as administrator, Hazel is helping to teach young children," said Mike.

"That's a challenge," said Libby.

"I was teaching third grade at a local school, but I'm finding this is a better fit for me," said Hazel.

"A happy choice for everyone, it seems," said Ray. "Now, let's get to it."

He led the way onto the court.

As Mike and Hazel went onto their side of the court together, he spoke softly to her. "Remember, if you don't think you can get a shot mid-court, I'll be there to back you up. If you can get it, let me know, and I'll stay out of the way."

She knew how much cooperation was needed to play on a doubles team. Though she and Mike hadn't practiced, she was determined to play her best.

Libby was a stronger player than Hazel and was very agile on her feet. Ray was an excellent server, but he was a little slow to move.

Mike, of course, was a professional player who seemed to fly like magic to get to a ball and whip it across the net.

As they each played, Mike encouraged them when he could.

Hazel's initial nervousness fled, and she settled into one of her most enjoyable games. Her body and mind seemed to remember past tournaments, and she sometimes returned a ball without much thought.

By the end of the set, the four were sweaty but smiling. Hazel noticed Elliott sitting with Craig and Tracy, watching from behind the fence. She gave him a little wave and mopped her brow.

"Okay," said Libby. "Let's cool off inside. I've brought hors d'oeuvres and a couple of pitchers of margaritas, so there should be plenty for us and our audience."

Hazel left the court with the others and stopped by the benches to speak to Elliott. "You three have been invited to join us for some drinks and appetizers. What do you think?"

Elliott glanced at the others. "I'm in."

Craig and Tracy agreed, and they all went inside to join the tennis group.

The Sports Center had not one lounge, but two. The first was in the main reception area where couches and chairs were scattered. The second, a smaller one, was by the kitchen and could be used for small group functions with tables and chairs.

Libby placed the appetizers on a table placed against a wall, and Ray set up a small bar area at the opposite end of the table.

After they'd all been served a drink and helped themselves to food, they took seats on the couches and chairs that formed a conversation circle at one end of the room.

Libby held up her paper cup. "Here's to a wonderful tennis match. Thank you, Mike and Hazel. It was such fun."

Ray, Mike, and Hazel raised their drinks. "A great time," said Ray.

"You all were outstanding," said Elliott. "It was enjoyable to watch."

Hazel smiled at him and noticed that Tracy looked put out. "I normally play with Mike," she told Libby and Ray. "Maybe we can do that sometime."

Mike shrugged. "This was an exciting teaching session. The group worked well together."

Tracy pressed her lips together, and Hazel was sure that wouldn't be the end of that conversation.

After some time, Hazel stood. "Thank you, everyone, for a delightful time. But I need to get home and get things ready for work tomorrow. My days usually start early."

"I heard you've been working with Jed Abbott, the foster child who's sparking a lot of interest. I admire that," said Libby.

"He's an extremely talented and very special boy. More than that, he's one of the sweetest kids I've ever met." Hazel's eyes stung with unexpected tears at the memory of how Jed had tried to take care of his family while Lisa was sick.

She shook hands with Libby and Ray, then turned to go.

"I'll go with you," said Elliott, getting to his feet.

They left together.

Outside, Elliott turned to her. "Are you all right?"

"Yes, thanks." They walked to her car. "I'm much more aware of children in foster care than I was before I met Jed. He's in a good home, but that isn't always the case. Even then, it's hard," said Hazel. "Though our families might be difficult sometimes, we're the lucky ones, aren't we?"

Elliott nodded. "Even now, when I know I might disappoint my parents in more ways than one, I do acknowledge that's what makes it so difficult. I've always known they wanted me to be happy, to have and do nice things, to carry on for the family. They've never understood how hard I tried."

"Have you had a chance to talk to Craig?" Hazel asked as they got into the car.

"Not yet, but he's going to show me Portsmouth. He likes going there," said Elliott.

"That's very nice of him. I'm sorry I'm so busy with work,"

Hazel said.

"It's fine. I don't want to put you to any trouble on my account. If it sounds fine to you, I bought a steak, and I'm willing to grill it up if you'll fix a salad for us."

"Oh, Elliott, that sounds perfect. After that tennis match, I'm hungry as a bear."

He laughed. "I'd forgotten you played tennis in high school and college. You're really good."

"It's starting to come back to me," said Hazel. "But I'll never be as talented as Mike, or maybe Tracy."

"What's up with her? She started to make a play for me and then realized I wasn't into her." Elliott shook his head. "I bet she's used to a lot of looks from the guys."

"She's beautiful," admitted Hazel. "And she has a fiery temper that's attractive when it isn't annoying."

"It looks like she and Mike are a couple. That's why you chose him to play the part of the man you're interested in, huh?"

"Yes. I just pray my mother doesn't come for a visit anytime soon. That would be a disaster," said Hazel, shuddering at the thought.

The evening with Elliott was fun. They were the best of friends, who could share history with a snort or a laugh at past experiences as they worked together on the meal.

Spending time with him, Hazel realized that when she was serious about a man in her life, she wanted someone with whom she was this comfortable. In social circles at home, there were a lot of pretenses. She was way beyond that.

After dinner, she and Elliott took a walk and

automatically ended up at the little garden that David Graham and his family had created.

Even as dusk was turning into darkness, they found the light from the street lamp to be enough to guide them to a bench near a small fountain.

The sound of trickling water, the cries of birds getting ready to settle for the night, and the sweet smell of nearby roses combined to give Hazel a sense of deep-felt peace.

She clasped Elliott's hand. "I believe things will work out for you. This is a pleasant place to get comfortable in your skin, as Craig might advise. Use the time here to make healthy decisions about your life going forward. What you're asking for is everyone's right—to be the person they are."

He gave her a questioning look. "Are you a better person here, like you want?"

"Yes," she said firmly. "I'm still finding myself in some ways, but here I feel I'm more open, more honest, freer to be me. The real me."

"That's what I want for myself. As long as I'm taking this break from my family, I want to make it last. Can you think of a job for me?"

"Your best bet is to ask Craig about it. He knows a lot of businesses in the area. You might even want to ask at one of the local credit unions."

"Something to think about," said Elliott. "Ready to go home?"

"Yes," she said, pleased that he felt so comfortable with her.

Later, when Elliott received a call from Craig confirming their day trip to Portsmouth, she was happy he already seemed to be making friends. But then, some small towns were like that. Lilac Lake was one of the best.

CHAPTER THIRTEEN

WHILE ELLIOTT USED THE NEXT FEW DAYS TO GET TO know Craig, hunt for a job, and relax, Hazel worked hard overseeing some new changes at the Sports Center. A new doubles tournament program was set up, providing an opportunity for people to meet, socialize, and work on improving their game.

The retail operation was growing fast. A store manager, a pleasant older woman, was brought in to help keep it on track.

And, as she and Evie from Access Sports in Concord had discussed, they worked together on setting up a second-hand store exchange for children to help families. Every person who participated was given a discount coupon to buy new clothes in Concord or at the store on-site.

Even though she was busy, Hazel still met with Jed every morning. Their sessions had become so much more than a chance to play tennis. A real bond was developing between them. Hazel encouraged Jed to talk about the future and what he hoped to accomplish.

Hazel thought about the possibility of adopting or fostering a child one day. The idea gave her a new reason to be careful who she might date in the future. It would take a special person to agree to such a plan.

One evening, Elliott greeted her at the cabin when she

came home from work and handed her a glass of champagne.

"What's this for?" Hazel asked. "Good news? Did you get a job?"

"Better than that. I came out to my parents. I had a Zoom call with them earlier this afternoon. I admit I was nervous, but as soon as I saw them on my computer screen, I knew I was doing the right thing. By doing it online, I kept things pretty calm. I explained this was nothing new, that I realized I was gay at an early age, but didn't want to disappoint them."

"How did they take it?" Hazel asked.

"My father got very quiet and wouldn't look into the camera. But my mother told me she'd love me no matter what. After my dad got off the call, she explained it would take him time to get used to the idea, but that he was a kind man and would come around. I don't think she realized her eyes were filled with tears the whole time I was talking."

"It sounds as if it went as well as it could. Your parents have had plans for you your whole life," said Hazel, hugging him. "I'm glad it's finally out in the open. Now, my parents will understand why marriage wasn't going to work for us."

"Yeah, I know. It made me realize how unfair I've been to you for not telling the truth earlier. I hope you forgive me for that."

"Of course, I do. I know what it's been like for you," Hazel said. "Any word on a job?"

Elliott shook his head. "Not yet. I have a meeting tomorrow with Brooks and Garth Beckman at their lumber company."

"Oh, that would be a perfect job for you," gushed Hazel. "Their business has grown by leaps and bounds, and I'm sure they could use a financial manager. I should've thought of that."

"We'll see," said Elliott. He raised his glass. "Let me enjoy the freedom I feel from telling my parents I'm gay, and that while you and I are going to continue to be best friends, we won't ever marry."

"Yes! I'll toast to that," said Hazel.

They went out to the deck with the bottle of champagne Elliott had bought to celebrate and sat enjoying the scenery and each other until it was time to go to Jake's for supper.

Before they could leave, Hazel's mother called her. "Hello, darling. I just heard from Elliott's mother. She was shocked by Elliott's news, but then realized she should've seen it earlier. We discussed the situation, and I told her I'd planned a trip north to see you this summer. I've been thinking I'll make that trip next week when Elliott is still there. You don't mind having another guest, do you?"

No! No! No! Hazel gasped and then forced herself to say calmly, "Why don't we see how things go with Elliott staying here? After he's acclimated here, you could come next month when the summer weather will be at its best. Elliott might have moved out of my house by then."

Elliott's eyes widened. He whispered, "Your mother? Here?"

"What do you think?" Hazel asked her mother.

Her mother sighed. "My social schedule is so full, I only have a limited opportunity to visit. I'll fly up on a Monday, after a Sunday golf tournament. Is that okay with you? I can stay at the Lilac Lake Inn if you can't accommodate me."

"How long do you plan to stay?" Hazel asked.

"I'll fly home on Friday. I don't want to miss out on a party that weekend. Does that timing work?" her mother asked.

Knowing she had no choice, Hazel said, "I'll see what I can do about finding a place for Elliott to stay so you can be here at the house with me."

"Okay, darling, that will do nicely. I'm anxious to see you. And a visit will give me time to get to know your new beau," her mother said, sending a wave of panic through Hazel. "Can't wait to see you. Love you."

"Love you, too," murmured Hazel, worried about the upcoming visit. She'd have to warn Mike.

At Jake's, Hazel was glad to see a big crowd. The only person Elliott hadn't met was Brooks Beckman. The fact he'd be meeting with Brooks tomorrow for an interview with Beckman Lumber made it that much more important.

Hazel waved to everyone and introduced Elliott to Brooks. Known as a cool guy who played guitar in a local band, Brooks was the younger brother of Garth Beckman. He did media work for the business.

Brooks was a handsome man in his early thirties with auburn hair and gray eyes who lit up at the sight of Elliott. "I understand my brother and I are going to meet with you tomorrow."

If Hazel didn't know Elliott as well as she did, she would've missed the gleam of interest he showed as he shook hands with Brooks.

Hazel studied them. Maybe things would work out better for Elliott than she'd thought. She'd hoped Elliott would find a place in town. Perhaps, business and friendship would both be available to him.

She turned as Mike and Tracy came into the bar. Tracy was still wearing a tennis dress, and every male eye watched as she walked toward them, aware she was on display.

Mike walked ahead, letting her take her time.

As Mike sat down beside her, Hazel quietly said, "We need to talk. My mother is coming to town next week."

He nodded and then pulled out the empty chair next to him for Tracy.

"Am I interrupting anything?" Tracy asked, glaring at Hazel.

"Not at all," Hazel said firmly. "Just some personal business."

Hazel and Elliott ordered drinks and food, and then Hazel leaned back in her chair and listened to others talk about their latest activities.

Ross announced that he'd arranged for kids to sign up to attend a Red Sox baseball game. He'd secured several seats and arranged transportation for an afternoon game.

Hazel made a mental note to ask Jed if he'd like to go.

Sarah and Dani told them they were supporting a youth baseball league at the Center.

Hazel listened, pleased to know that the Sports Center was having such an impact on life in Lilac Lake. From across the table, Ross looked at her and winked. She'd met with him earlier that day, and he'd told her they were giving her a raise.

When Hazel was ready to go home, she turned to Elliott. "I'm ready to leave. Are you?"

He shook his head. "I'll stay a while longer. Brooks told me he'd give me a ride home."

Hazel saw the happiness on his face. "Okay, I'll leave the front porch light on."

The next morning, when Hazel arrived at the tennis court, Jed was sitting on the bench holding his head in his hands. She approached and quietly sat beside him.

"Everything okay?" she asked gently.

He lifted his face and shook his head. "Lucinda is sick."

"Is she going to be okay?" Hazel asked.

Jed shrugged. "Lisa is taking care of her, but Lucinda has what Lisa says are serious health issues."

Hazel put an arm across his shoulders. "I'm sorry to hear this. If you need me to help, please let me know."

His eyes shining, he said, "I will. Lisa says Lucinda likes me best because I can make her smile."

"It's nice that Lucinda knows you care," said Hazel. "That's important. No matter what happens."

Mike approached. "Are we ready?"

Jed jumped to his feet. "I am."

Hazel rose, aware that Jed was embarrassed by his previous tears.

CHAPTER FOURTEEN

AFTER HAZEL PLAYED TENNIS WITH JED AND MIKE, SHE decided to walk Jed home. She wanted to see if there was anything she could do to help Lisa with Lucinda. She couldn't imagine having a foster child who needed so much care. She'd seen an array of machinery and medical equipment to know how underdeveloped Lucinda was.

When she and Jed got to the house, a car was parked in front of it.

Jed raced up the porch steps ahead of her and entered the house.

Hazel followed behind, hoping she wasn't intruding.

A woman wearing a nurse's scrubs stood with Lisa, checking Lucinda.

Lisa saw her and acknowledged Hazel with a bob of her head and then put an arm around Jed.

"Lucinda is going to the hospital. She has pneumonia and can't breathe well on her own," said Lisa to both of them, a look of worry etched on her face. "The nurse has called the EMTs, and I'll ride with Lucinda to the Portsmouth Hospital, where she can get the best help possible. I've called Janis, next door, but she's out and won't be here for half an hour or so. Hazel, will you stay here with Harry and Baby Simon?"

"Yes, of course. And Jed will help me, won't you?" Hazel asked him, knowing how important it was for him to keep busy.

"Yes. I'll take care of them too," he said.

"They're both down for morning naps but should be getting up soon," said Lisa, carefully wrapping Lucinda in a blanket and groaning softly as she lifted her into her arms.

Seeing Lisa carrying what looked like a very large baby, tears came to Hazel's eyes.

The EMTs talked to the nurse and checked Lucinda, who lay lethargically in Lisa's arms. Then they led Lisa to the back of the ambulance and put them both inside where they could monitor Lucinda on the way to the hospital.

As the ambulance moved away from the curb, Hazel placed a hand on Jed's shoulder. "She's getting the best help she can."

From the house, Hazel heard a baby crying. "C'mon, Jed. We have work to do." She didn't want him to spend the next few hours worrying. The situation was out of their hands.

Harry met them at the doorway, holding onto a blanket and sucking his thumb. From a room in the back of the house, Hazel heard the baby crying.

"Jed, take Harry to the kitchen and have him sit at the table in his booster seat. I'll be back with the baby."

"Harry needs his diaper changed," said Jed.

"Okay, but let me check on the baby first," said Hazel. She walked into the baby's room and saw him sitting up in his crib. He stopped crying and stared at her.

"It's okay, Simon, I'm here to help you," Hazel crooned. She went over to the crib, lifted him, and realized he'd soaked through his diaper onto the little shirt he was wearing.

Knowing she had no choice, she laid Simon on a changing

table, and talking softly to him, struggled to change his diaper and clean him up.

Staring at her, he alternated between being fascinated and wanting to cry.

Hazel hadn't realized she was making all sorts of noises to keep Simon's attention until Jed, standing at the doorway, said, "What are you doing?"

"I'm trying my best to get him changed," said Hazel. "Can you grab me a fresh shirt for me?"

Jed handed the shirt to her, "Get his head through it first, then his arms."

"Thanks," said Hazel, wondering how often Jed had changed Simon's clothes.

Once she was done, she headed to the kitchen with both boys.

"I gave Harry some Cheerios," said Jed. "Lisa gives him some fruit in the morning, but I'm not allowed to use a knife."

"Okay, I'll take care of it," said Hazel, placing Simon in a highchair. At almost a year old, Simon was excited to have some Cheerios too.

Hazel found a half box of strawberries in the refrigerator and cut some up for both little boys. "How about you, Jed? Do you want a snack?"

"Can I have a banana?" he asked, pointing to a bunch sitting on the counter.

"I'm sure Lisa won't mind," Hazel said, impressed by the food choices. "Do you always have fruit around?"

Jed nodded. Lisa is a nutra ...nutritionis ...

"Oh, a nutritionist. That's nice." A thought struck her. "Is Lisa a nurse too?"

"Sometimes," said Jed. "She and Janis help each other."

Hazel was sitting in the kitchen with the three boys when Janis arrived. "Hi, I got the message about Lucinda and got here as quickly as I could. I'll take over."

"Thanks," said Hazel. "I've changed Simon, but Harry hasn't had a diaper change after his nap. Jed says it needs changing, but Harry was eating his snack, and I didn't want to disturb him."

"No problem. I'll do it when he's ready," said Janis.

"I'm going to return to the Sports Center, but will you please keep me informed?" Hazel asked her.

"I will," said Janis.

Hazel gave Jed a quick hug. "If you need me, you know where I am."

"I know," he said and turned away, but not before she saw his eyes fill.

Even as her heart went out to him, she headed for the Center.

That afternoon, Hazel was working in the retail shop, doing a quick inventory, when her cell phone rang. *Lisa.*

"Hello," said Hazel, her heart pumping with worry. "What's up?"

Hazel heard a sob, and then Lisa said, "It's Lucinda. She suffered what they think is heart failure, perhaps due to the stress on her body. She died before we could get her to the hospital."

"That's awful," said Hazel. "Simply awful. What can I do?"

"Lucinda lived longer than anyone thought she would. But I'm worried about Jed. He's taking it hard. He left the house, and I think he's on his way to see you."

"Okay, I'll head outside now," Hazel said. "Thanks for the call. I'll keep in touch."

"I've got to go," Hazel told the store manager and hurried outside, hoping she could catch Jed before he reached the Center.

Hazel jogged in the direction of Jed's house and saw him approach the baseball field. She increased her pace and met him by the bleachers.

"Hi, Jed," Hazel said putting her arms around him. "Lisa just called me and told me about Lucinda. I'm so sorry."

Jed leaned into her and sobbed. The sound of his pain was heartbreaking.

After he quieted, Hazel led him to the empty bleachers, and they sat together.

"I should have helped her more," said Jed, biting his lips together.

Hazel placed an arm around him and gave him a squeeze of sympathy. "When someone is that sick, they can't always be saved. Lisa told me that Lucinda lived longer than anyone thought she would. Maybe you helped with that."

"Lisa said Lucinda loved me best," Jed said, staring into the empty ballfield. "Why did she have to die?"

"I don't know," Hazel said. "Though she's not living in the house with you anymore, she can still be in your thoughts and heart for as long as you let her."

Jed gazed up at her thoughtfully.

Hazel's heart went out to him. He was such a special boy.

Ross came onto the baseball field, saw them, and jogged over as fast as his past-injured knees would let him.

"Hey, there! What's going on?"

Hazel introduced Jed to Ross and explained that he used to play for the New York Yankees.

Jed's eyes rounded. "Wow! I like the Red Sox, but I can like the Yankees too."

Ross chuckled and tousled Jed's hair. "I hear you're an excellent tennis player."

Jed glanced at Hazel. "I really like tennis."

"Keep up the good work. We're going to have a practice ballgame soon. You're welcome to come watch us anytime," Ross told Jed.

"Thanks," said Jed, getting to his feet. "I've got to go home. Lisa needs me."

Hazel leaned over to hug him, and his arms wrapped around her waist. "Call me anytime you need to talk," she said. "I hope to see you tomorrow."

She watched him trot away and sank onto the bleachers, unaware Mike was approaching her.

She whipped around when she heard him say, "Hi, Hazel. What's going on?"

He took a seat next to her and gave her a look of concern.

"It's Lucinda ..." She didn't realize she was crying until Mike thumbed a tear from her cheek. "Her heart couldn't take anymore. Lisa called to tell me Jed was taking it hard and was coming to talk to me. I met him here."

"Aw, I'm sorry," said Mike. "Another bad break for Jed. I heard you were at the house this morning to help Lisa. That was so nice of you."

"I really admire Lisa. She apparently does or has done some nursing, and Jed mentioned her being a nutritionist.

She must have a heart of gold to foster kids, especially kids like Lucinda."

"Lisa and her husband are doing an exceptional job with Jed," said Mike.

"I think if I ever marry, I'd want not only kids of my own but children who may need a home," said Hazel.

Mike studied her but didn't say anything.

In the silence that followed, Hazel remembered her mother's upcoming visit. She faced Mike. "I need to talk to you about my mother's visit. Are you going to be able to help me? You don't have to pretend to be too serious about me. Just show enough interest that my mother will believe we're at least dating."

Mike's mouth twitched with humor. "I might be able to do that."

"I don't know whether we should tell Tracy about the arrangement. If she finds out, she won't be sympathetic," said Hazel.

"Leave her to me," said Mike. "She'll have to deal with it."

"I don't want to do anything to hurt your relationship with her. I know how important you are to her."

"How so?" Mike asked.

Hazel squirmed. She'd feel very uncomfortable telling him that Tracy liked that he was important in the tennis world and wanted to use that to help her.

"Never mind," said Mike, frowning as Tracy called him.

While Mike headed to Tracy to talk to her, Hazel walked away, wondering how things would work out. Lying was never a good idea, and now she had to pay for it.

CHAPTER FIFTEEN

AFTER WORK, HAZEL PULLED INTO HER DRIVEWAY READY for some downtime with Elliott. He'd been asleep when she left the house that morning, and she wondered how last night with Brooks had gone, as well as his interview at Beckman Lumber.

Elliott met her at the door. "I thought I heard your car." He handed her a glass of red wine. "Come in, sit down, and relax. I've picked up dinner from the Lilac Café, so you don't have to do anything about a meal."

"Wow! How marvelous. It's been a rough day." She accepted the glass of wine and walked into the kitchen and out onto the deck. The deck was her refuge at home unless the weather dictated otherwise. Tonight was pleasant after a cool front had entered the area with the promise of rain later in the evening.

"How did your meeting go at Beckman Lumber?" she asked Elliott.

Elliott's face lit with excitement. "It went well. I can easily do the job they're offering and still have time for other work. Craig and I are talking about opening a financial consulting business together. He has several clients, and Beckman Lumber will be my first client. I already have leads on a couple of other small businesses in the area who might be able to use my help. Rather than working for someone else, I would be working for myself. That's a very appealing idea."

Hazel let out a puff of satisfaction. "That's even better than I'd hoped."

"I can start with Beckman Lumber right away," said Elliott. "The rest will take time to develop. But I'm very excited about it."

"And how about Brooks? I thought I detected a note of interest there," said Hazel.

"That, too, is something that might develop someday. He and I have a lot in common, and he's really nice, very discreet."

"I think I see a chance for you to move here permanently. Is this what you're talking about?"

Elliott grinned. "Your group of friends is the best. Poppy will be moving out of her cabin in the next few weeks. I've already agreed to take over her lease. In the meantime, Craig said I could bunk with him for a while. He has a guestroom that isn't often used."

"All these decisions in a matter of days. I'm impressed," said Hazel. "It takes a small town like this to make it work."

"That's for sure. Everyone knows someone who knows something. Amazing," said Elliott, chuckling.

"I'm so relieved for you. Being open about yourself has already made you some new friends," Hazel said.

Elliott gave her a thoughtful look. "Tell me about your day."

Hazel took a sip of wine and set down her glass. "It was tough. Jed lost a foster sibling when her heart gave out. She was a child with many health issues and wasn't expected to live very long. But Jed was very kind to Lucinda, helping her to exercise in the hopes that she would walk one day."

Hazel took a deep breath to calm her emotions.

Elliott handed her a cocktail napkin to wipe her tears.

She took it, dabbed her eyes with it, and continued. "It's made me realize a lot of things about myself and the life I hope to have."

"What do you mean?" Elliott asked.

"I've wanted a family someday, but now I think I want to include a child that might not be my own. Someone who needs a loving home. Like Jed."

"You've always been kind, Hazel. Maybe, this is a way to continue that," said Elliott. "But first, don't you think you'd better find a mate? It would make it a lot easier."

Hazel chuckled at his teasing look. "I guess I'm getting way ahead of myself. But I have Mike agreeing to make my mother think we might be dating. That's a first step."

"He seems like a likable guy who's being a good sport about helping you. But I don't think his girlfriend, Tracy, will be pleased. She doesn't seem like the sharing type."

"You're right, which is why Mike and I need to be careful." She held up her empty glass. "How about a refill? I want to toast a little girl named Lucinda."

Elliott left and quickly returned with the bottle of wine and a can of peanuts.

After he refilled their glasses and handed her the peanuts, he sat in his chair, gazing at her. "We've known one another all our lives, but I believe this is the first time we've both stated exactly what each of us wants for the future without filtering it through others' expectations."

Hazel smiled and lifted her glass. "Here's to us. We're finally growing up."

Elliott laughed and saluted her with his wineglass. "You could say we're late bloomers. It's taken us a while to understand what we want from life on many levels."

"I have plenty of time to make my plans come true. As you said, I don't even have a boyfriend," said Hazel. "And right now, I'm not looking."

"Probably just as well," said Elliott. "I'm impressed by how busy you are at your job. Your father would be proud of all your skills."

Hazel snorted. "But my mother would be disappointed if she knew I'm not considering any serious relationship. And now that I know what I want in a family, I'm not likely to find anyone who shares my views. Not easily, anyway."

"Listen, we have a few days before your mother comes, let's just enjoy ourselves," said Elliott. "I heard there's a superb Mexican place outside of town. Are you up for that?"

"Yes, but I also want to go with you to Stan's for some delicious seafood. Maybe we can do that tomorrow night."

"Deal."

"Tonight, I'm too tired to do anything else but enjoy the food you brought home," said Hazel. She couldn't get memories of Jed's sad face out of her mind.

"Just relax. I'll take care of everything."

Hazel took Elliott at his word, sat back in her chair, and lifted her feet onto the deck railing, telling herself she deserved some downtime. Elliott wasn't really company but a friend staying with her for a while.

Later, when Elliott suggested they go to Jake's, Hazel shook her head. "You go. I'm off to bed to read. It's the only way for me to relax before going to sleep, and I have to get up early."

After seeing him off, she picked up the book she was reading and headed to her bedroom.

Her cell phone rang. *Her mother.*

Hazel let it go to voicemail. She still had a lot of thinking to do before she faced her mother's usual questions.

After she got ready, she climbed into bed, picked up her book, but laid it down, her thoughts whirling. Tomorrow, she'd ask Lisa what she could do to help both her and Jed. The absence of Lucinda's presence and her constant needs would leave a huge hole behind. They'd worked hard to help her the best they could.

The next morning, Hazel went to the tennis courts, unsure whether Jed would be there. But as she approached, she saw him sitting on a bench, his head in his hands. She called, and he lifted his head and gave her a little wave.

"How are you doing today?" she asked him, sitting down beside him.

Jed shrugged. "It's very quiet in the house with Lucinda gone."

"Oh, yes. We're all sad about it. You can talk to me about her anytime you want."

He stood and picked up his racket.

Hazel got to her feet, and they went onto the court.

Their game was one of the best they've ever played, with serves going in and balls being returned.

Hazel had no idea they were being watched until after a long rally between them, with her winning the point, Hazel heard the sound of clapping and turned to see Mike.

"You both are doing great," said Mike, beaming at them.

"Yeah, but Hazel beat me," said Jed.

"That, my man, is no reason to be upset," said Mike. "You played well. We can work on any improvements together."

Hazel walked over to the fence to grab her towel and wipe down her face.

"Can we talk?" asked Mike, coming up beside her.

"Sure, give me a chance to cool down," said Hazel.

Mike chatted with Jed, and then Jed took off for home with a promise to call if Lisa needed help.

"You really care about him, don't you?" said Mike.

"I do," Hazel answered. "Knowing him has opened my eyes to many things."

Mike followed her off the court to a bench and sat down beside her.

"I told Tracy about our arrangement when your mother comes for a visit. She was upset until I explained to her that neither one of us had any interest in the other. Right?" His green-eyed gaze rested on her.

A stab of disappointment made her feel off-balance. Hazel studied the man she'd come to admire. That was the deal. Just friends. "You can tell her she has no reason to worry."

"Okay, but just so you know, I'm sure she'll be watching us closely," said Mike. He kept his gaze on her and then got to his feet. "Are you available for another doubles match as part of training?"

"Sure, that was a lot of fun," said Hazel. "Though Elliott is staying with me, we're pretty much on our own, except tonight we're going to Stan's to hear some music and get some seafood. Want to join us?"

"Thanks, but Tracy has already made plans for us," said Mike.

"Maybe another time," said Hazel, thinking Misty and David might like to join them.

When Hazel got to her office, she called Misty and they quickly arranged to meet at Stan's at seven o'clock that evening. Landscapers tended to work late hours in the summer, Misty explained, but she and David needed a break.

Satisfied they had a pleasant evening ahead, she called Elliott to give him the plans.

"Okay," he said. "Brooks is playing there tonight with another guitar player and a singer. He wanted me to come and see him perform."

"That makes it even more fun," said Hazel, pleased that Elliott was forming friendships.

After work, Hazel raced home to freshen up and change for the first night out of town in what had seemed a long time.

Wanting to be able to learn where things were, Elliott drove.

When he pulled into a dirt parking lot outside a rustic, wooden, one-story building painted red and sitting next to a narrow stream, Elliott turned to Hazel. "This is it?"

She laughed. "It isn't fancy, but they have the best fried clams and fresh lobster around."

They got out of the car and walked toward the building.

A colorful metal sign tacked by the front door advertised seafood and craft beer. Above the door, a carved wooden sign said "Stan's".

Inside, a bar lined one end of the room. The bar stools in

front of it were mostly filled. The other end of the room held several four-top tables with red-checkered plastic tablecloths, adding to the casual atmosphere.

The side wall contained a small stage where a piano sat. Tonight, sound equipment was set up for the expected singer and two guitar players. There was no sign of Brooks, but it was early for his performance.

Elliott and Hazel sat at a table with an excellent view of the stage.

A young waitress wearing denim cut-off shorts and a red T-shirt came over to take their orders.

"Any specials?" asked Elliott.

"If you haven't had our fried lobster or clam chowder, you're in for a treat. Other than that, everything on the menu is really tasty, I promise you."

"Ah, in that case, let me look over the menu." He turned to Hazel. "Want a beer or something stronger?"

"I'll take a Hampshire light ale," said Hazel. She knew she'd have the fried lobster. She could already taste the sweet meat with a butter and lemon dipping sauce.

"Same for me," said Elliott to the waitress. "I see you're busy, so I'll decide on my meal soon."

After the waitress left, Elliott said, "Any recommendations for dinner?"

"A New England dish called 'scrod' is always delicious. It's a baked cod dish that, done right, is delicious. Other than that, I'd recommend lobster, clams, or fish and chips. As the waitress said, Stan's is all about excellent food and music."

"Okay, I'll try the scrod." He looked around. "This is a happening place."

"It'll be even busier when it's time for the music," said Hazel.

Their beers came, and as they were waiting for their food, Mike showed up.

"What are you doing here? Where's Tracy?" Hazel asked him as he sat at their table.

"She and I fought. I thought I'd give her some space," Mike answered. "I hope your invitation still stands."

"Sure. Misty and David are joining us too, but there's always room for more."

"I can go if it's too crowded," said Mike.

"No way," said Elliott. He signaled the waitress, and when she came over, Mike ordered a beer.

They were chatting comfortably when Misty and David arrived.

Hazel watched them walk across the room. David was gently guiding Misty by her elbow and helping her weave through the tables. Hazel thought they were adorable together.

Elliott and Mike stood as Misty and David reached them, and then, after shaking hands with David, the four of them sat down.

"Where's Tracy?" asked Misty.

Mike sighed. "She's not coming. Hope you don't mind an extra."

"Not at all. This will give me a chance to get to know you better," said Misty. "Until now, you've been pretty much working in Florida."

"Yes, I teach tennis there in the winter months, but the program is growing so fast here at the Sports Center that I may stay on for the winter crowd that we're trying to create here."

Hazel shot Mike a look of confusion, and he smiled.

Misty, David, and Mike ordered dinner, and soon they were all eating together.

"Service here is quick," commented Elliott. "No wonder this place is so popular."

"It's been here forever," said David. "They thought about tearing the place down and building something bigger, fancier, and decided not to. I'm glad. This is one-of-a-kind in this area."

"Hazel took me to your family park," said Elliott. "It's beautiful."

David smiled a little sadly. "My sister was a wonderful person. Far too young to die."

"And very nice, very beautiful," added Misty.

"I haven't seen it," Mike admitted. "I'll have to go there sometime."

"I'll take you anytime," said Hazel. "It's not far from my house, and I stop there quite often."

"I hear you're doing some work for Beckman Lumber," said Misty, looking at Elliott. "How's that going?"

"Excellent," said Elliott. "I'm going into business with Craig Evans, and Beckman Lumber is my primary customer at this point."

"I'm very proud and pleased that Elliott is settling in so quickly," said Hazel.

Misty took a sip of beer and then blurted, "You were supposed to marry Hazel?"

Taken aback by Misty's boldness, Elliott and Hazel looked at one another.

Hazel remained quiet, wondering what Elliott would say.

"As much as I love Hazel, it wasn't going to happen," said Elliott. "I'm gay."

Misty bobbed her head. "That's a smart decision, then."

Hazel couldn't help chuckling at Misty's earnest expression, and soon they were all laughing, relieving the tension.

Mike gave her a steady look.

Hazel cleared her throat. "You might as well be in on the plan, everyone. Mike has agreed to pretend to be dating me when my mother comes to visit me in a couple of days. To get her off my back about Elliott, I blurted out that I had a boyfriend in town. When my mother grilled me, the only single guy I could think of was Mike." Hazel shook her head. "It's all a horrible mistake, but thankfully, Mike's helping me out."

"Y'all don't know how a Southern mother can be about wanting her children settled with a family," said Elliott. "Like our two mothers."

"I'm hoping her visit will simply be fun and harmless," said Hazel. "We'll see."

Elliott gave her a skeptical look.

CHAPTER SIXTEEN

Hazel's mother had conveniently flown into Portsmouth International Airport rather than having Hazel pick her up in Boston. It didn't mean that Hazel was any less anxious about meeting her mother and taking her to Lilac Lake.

When she saw her mother walk across the terminal toward her, unexpected tears stung Hazel's eyes. For all the friction between them, there was love.

In her fifties, her mother's blonde hair, svelte figure, and lovely pink dress caught the attention of others.

Hazel waved and moved forward for a hug.

"Hi, Mom. How was the trip?"

"The flight to Boston was delayed, and then I almost missed the one to here. So, I'm ready to get to your place and get comfortable, maybe have a glass of wine. I hope you don't have anything planned for tonight. I'd like to relax a bit. It feels like forever since you've been home."

Hazel looped her arm through her mother's, and they went to the luggage carousel.

Looking at the two large suitcases her mother had brought, Hazel tensed. This was supposed to be a short visit.

"How long are you planning to stay?" Hazel asked.

Her mother chuckled. "Don't worry. I packed one of my suitcases with stuff from your room at home. As long as you've declared this is where you're going to be living, I thought I'd change your bedroom into my exercise room."

'Oh, well, that makes sense," said Hazel, feeling as if she'd been kicked out. Knowing she was being silly, she rolled one suitcase ahead of her mother and led her to her blue VW convertible.

"It's handy that the top is down," said Hazel. "We'll put the suitcases in the backseat."

Her mother lifted a scarf out of her handbag.

"Prepared as always," said Hazel.

Her mother smiled and wrapped the scarf around her head. "I try to be ready for anything."

Hazel loaded the suitcases and then climbed behind the wheel while her mother settled in the passenger seat.

"I've sent you photographs of Lilac Lake, but they don't do justice to the real thing," said Hazel as she pulled out of the parking lot. "I'm hoping while you're here, you'll understand why I'm so content."

"I'm anxious to see what it's all about, including your young man," her mother said.

Hazel turned to her mother. "He's not my young man. We're just dating without it being too serious."

"I'm still curious as to who has caught your attention, especially now that Elliott is out of the picture." Her mother shook her head. "I promised Cassandra I'd spend some time with her son. She's struggling with all of his life decisions. Both his parents are."

"I've never seen him so happy," said Hazel. "He's already made friends and is busy setting up his partnership with the man who serves as Financial Director for the Sports Center. It's a fantastic opportunity for him."

As Hazel drove through town, her mother gaped at the scenery on both sides of Main Street. "Why, this is … precious! Postcards and photos don't do this town justice."

"Even better, the people behind the beautiful storefronts and restaurants make the town very special," said Hazel, feeling a sense of pride over the town she'd adopted as her own.

As she'd done with Elliott, she admired the colorful awnings over the entrances to shops whose windows were filled with colorful displays of the tempting wares inside.

"What a cute idea to hang baskets of flowers from the decorative lamp posts," said her mother.

"You should see the town at Christmas," said Hazel. "Wreaths hang from the lamp posts, and they're wrapped with white lights. All the pots outside the store contain greens and ornaments. It's very charming."

"If I had realized all that, I wouldn't have insisted you come home for the holidays," said her mother. "Maybe with your boyfriend living here, I can convince your father to come to Lilac Lake for Christmas."

"Mom, please don't count on anything happening between Mike Dawson and me. We're just dating," said Hazel, recognizing the panic in her voice. This whole situation could become an embarrassing episode in her life. Even Mike was concerned about the complication with Tracy.

Hazel drove to her cabin and parked the car in the driveway. Elliott's car was absent, letting her know he'd gone to Craig's house until he could move into Poppy's cabin.

"Isn't this pretty?" said her mother, gazing at the cabin. "It looks very … cozy."

"It's perfect for me," Hazel said. Her parents' home seemed palatial compared to the cabin, but she loved it.

Hazel got both bags inside and led her mother to the guest room. "You have a nice view of the woods and the river," she said, hoisting a bag onto a luggage rack.

"Oh, how sweet! You've placed fresh flowers in the room for me," said her mother.

Hazel smiled. "I thought you'd like them."

"Oh, yes, zinnias are so colorful." Her mother gazed out the window. "Lovely."

"I'll give you time to get yourself settled, and then we can sit on the deck with a glass of wine," said Hazel. "Anything I can do for you?"

"No, thanks. I'll take care of a few things and then meet you outside."

Hazel left her mother, pleased that things seemed off to a comfortable start. She'd arranged for Mike to stop by before going out to dinner with Tracy. She was curious to see how that would go.

She set out nuts and olives for snacks and pulled a chilled bottle of pinot grigio from the refrigerator. Knowing her mother might be tired from making the trip, she'd planned to have a simple supper at home.

When her mother walked into the kitchen, she was smiling. "This is an attractive little place for you for the moment. You said friends of yours are building beautiful homes outside of town. That might be a smart investment for you or you and Mike together. When do I get to meet this man of yours?"

"He's going to stop by before attending a business

meeting," said Hazel. "Tomorrow, he'll come for dinner. I thought the two of us would have a simple meal to give you time to relax."

"That's thoughtful, thank you." Her mother sniffed the air. "The scent of pine is always refreshing. "

"I love hearing and seeing the birds," said Hazel. "It's so peaceful."

"Tell me about your job. And you mentioned a sweet little boy who plays tennis with you."

"Jed Abbott is the sweetest boy I've ever met. He's in foster care and living with a family in town. It's given me a reason to think about my future. Someday, I'd like to consider adopting or fostering a child. Seeing how much need there is for it, it's a wonderful thing to do."

"Don't you think you're rushing it a bit? Have you and Mike talked about this?" asked her mother.

"Our relationship isn't like that," said Hazel, hoping the whole visit wasn't going to be about her mother putting her and Mike together.

As if he knew the trouble she was in, Mike rang the doorbell on schedule. At least, she assumed that's who it was.

Relieved, she went to answer it.

He stood there gazing around.

"I'm so glad to see you," said Hazel, opening the door and standing back so he could enter.

"Remember, I can't stay. Tracy has made plans for us to meet up with a couple from the Sports Center," said Mike. "A business deal."

"I've explained that you have a business meeting to attend," said Hazel.

Mike gave her an approving look. "This couple is in the doubles group and is important to the Center."

Hazel led Mike out to the deck and introduced him to her mother.

After shaking hands politely, Mike took a seat next to her mother.

As they talked, Hazel had a chance to assess Mike. After working with so many people helping them to play tennis, he had an easy way about him. The fact that he was athletic and had striking features with brown hair pulled back into a sexy ponytail and green eyes that flashed with friendliness made him appealing.

Hazel grimaced as her mother asked Mike, "So, who is your family and where do they come from?"

Mike hesitated and sat straighter. "I have no idea who or where they are. I've been raised in foster homes."

"Oh." Hazel's mother blinked in surprise. "I suppose that's where Hazel gets the idea of you two adopting or fostering children one day."

Mike shot Hazel a look.

"Mother, please, I said that Mike and I were just dating," said Hazel, her cheeks burning.

Mike remained quiet, and Hazel quickly took over the conversation talking about her job at the Sports Center, and how Mike was the tennis pro there.

The time for Mike to leave couldn't come fast enough.

When he checked his watch, Hazel jumped to her feet. "Is it time? You don't want to be late for your meeting."

He gave her a look of relief. "Yes, I'd better go. It was very nice meeting you, Mrs. Belmont."

"Likewise," her mother said, smiling at him.

Hazel walked Mike to the door. "Sorry about all that. Hopefully, we can fill the conversation with other things."

"It was very interesting," said Mike. "See you tomorrow."

He surprised her by leaning over and kissing her on the cheek.

Hazel returned to her mother.

"Mike seems like a decent man, but, darling, no family, a tennis pro?" Her mother's gaze was disapproving.

"No matter what happens between Mike and me, I know he's a good guy who's worked hard to become the man he is. I will never forget that." Hazel spoke firmly and reached up to touch the spot on her cheek where he'd kissed her.

CHAPTER SEVENTEEN

THE NEXT MORNING, HAZEL DROVE TO THE SPORTS Center, eager for a workout with Jed. She'd thought about the sweet kiss Mike had given her and how she'd so quickly responded to her mother's thoughts about Mike and realized she'd come to really like him.

Both of her parents had come from wealthy backgrounds, so they didn't understand what it was like to make something of yourself from nothing. And, Lisa's raising foster children, one of whom was not expected to live long, would shame her mother for her easy acceptance of a life Lisa would never have.

She parked her car, headed to the courts, and was glad to see Jed waiting for her.

She waved and walked over to him. "' Morning. How are you?"

He shrugged, and a frown furrowed his brow. "Lisa's sad. She told me we might have to move."

"Move? Away from here?" Hazel asked, feeling sick.

"I don't know," said Jed. "She was talking to someone else."

"Oh, well, I'll talk to Lisa. I'm sure it's nothing for you to worry about," said Hazel, hoping that was true.

They went onto the court and began to play.

Soon, all thoughts but those about the game disappeared as Jed gave as good as she did, keeping the ball flying over the net back and forth.

When they were through, Hazel gave Jed a high-five. "We're getting better."

Jed smiled and nodded. "Mike thinks so too."

"I've got a busy day, but if you need me to talk to Lisa, please call me," Hazel said to Jed.

"Okay," he replied and trotted away.

Watching him leave, Hazel frowned. She'd sure miss Jed if he moved away, or did it mean he'd be reassigned to a different foster home? The thought sent acid to her stomach.

She went into the building to change for work. She was taking her mother to lunch at the Lilac Lake Café and then would give her a tour of the Sports Center. In the meantime, she had work to do.

The morning flew by as Hazel reviewed schedules for the various sports activities, posted new ones, reviewed employee schedules, and worked on marketing ideas.

When Hazel drove home to pick up her mother, she was ready for a break.

"I've had a lovely, lazy morning," said her mother. "But I'm looking forward to lunch."

"The food at the Café is excellent. My friend, Crystal, used to own it, but now she helps her husband with his medical practice."

As they headed back into town, Hazel swung by the Grahams' small park and explained how the family had given it to the town in memory of their daughter, David's sister.

"Such a sweet idea," said her mother.

"After lunch, we can stroll up and down Main Street. I'm sure you'll find plenty of things in the shops that you'll like," said Hazel. "And, of course, I want to give you a tour of the Sports Center."

"Can't wait," said her mother. "Of all the jobs I imagined for you, I could never envision you at a sports facility, playing and helping to teach tennis."

"You're going to be impressed," said Hazel confidently. It was so much more than ordinary.

Hazel parked the car and led her mother into the café.

"Where do you want to sit? It's pleasant enough to sit outside," said Hazel.

"Outside will be lovely," said her mother. "It's so much cooler here than at home."

As they stepped onto the patio, Hazel saw Ross Roberts sitting with one of the other owners of the Inn. She waved to him and sat down at a table not far away.

"Is that Ross Roberts, the ex-baseball star?" her mother.

"Yes, he's married to my friend, Melissa, and is part owner of the Inn. He's a super delightful guy," said Hazel.

A waitress came over to hand them menus and fill their water glasses." Nice to see you, Hazel."

"Thanks, this is my mother, Helena Belmont," said Hazel.

"Welcome to Lilac Lake. You'll love it here, if even for only a visit," the older waitress said.

"It's delightful already," said Hazel's mother.

After some discussion, Hazel and her mother each ordered a chicken salad plate garnished with a summer fruit selection and iced lemonade.

As they sat eating, several other people waved to Hazel as they went in and out of the café.

"You certainly know a lot of people," said her mother.

Hazel chuckled. "Small town living. At first, it took some getting used to, but now I love it."

"It reminds me a little bit of home because as big as the area is, we tend to stick to our crowd," said her mother.

"You're busy as ever with all the social activities. How's Dad? Still at the top of his golf game at the club?" asked Hazel.

"Oh, yes. It's important that he has that physical activity. It keeps him from getting too restless. I can't imagine what it will be like when the time comes for him to retire. Even though it's at least ten years or more off, I'm all for keeping him at his job."

"I don't blame you," said Hazel, chuckling. "It's good that he has his hunting and fishing buddies, too." Her father was a social person, as well.

After lunch, as promised, Hazel led her mother up and down Main Street, stopping at whatever shops interested her mother.

Sometime later, they headed over to the Sports Center.

When they pulled up to the sprawling, brick-faced building, Hazel's mother gasped. "I had no idea it was so big."

"It has everything. An indoor and outdoor pool, tennis and pickleball courts, a baseball diamond and a baseball training facility, an indoor climbing wall, basketball courts in and out, and the normal gym and training facilities."

As they walked inside, Hazel explained, "The vision is for year-round opportunities for sports enthusiasts to find something available right here in town. In the winter, skiers may look for a change of pace at our center. The Inn is working on special marketing with us for their guests."

"With all the different programs, it sounds like the whole town will be part of it," said her mother.

"Yes, the county made a deal for Ross and Mike to buy the land," said Hazel. "They've come through with all they promised."

"I'm impressed," said her mother.

A young woman behind the welcome desk spoke to them cheerfully when they walked inside. "Welcome to the Sports Center. May I help you, Hazel?"

"I'm showing my mother the entire operation here. Thank you for asking," said Hazel sincerely. It had taken several training sessions to make sure the young students handling the front desk understood the importance of greeting visitors.

"I'll show you my office," said Hazel. "It's not fancy but is nicely laid out."

As they headed down the hall, Craig Evans approached them. "Afternoon, Hazel."

"Craig, meet my mother, Helena Belmont. She's visiting me for a couple of days."

"Yes, that's why Elliott moved in with me," said Craig. "Welcome to Lilac Lake, Ms. Belmont."

"Thank you. It's such a lovely little town. You say Elliott is staying with you? I'm hoping to meet up with him. I promised his mother I'd spend some time with him and see how he's doing."

Hazel and Craig exchanged knowing glances.

"I've already arranged for Elliott to have dinner with us one night," said Hazel.

"Oh, that's good then," said Craig. "See you later. I'm off to a business appointment." He turned to Hazel's mother.

"Enjoy your stay."

"Thank you," her mother said. "I will."

"Craig is the person Elliott is going into business with. He's very agreeable and very smart. He's started a successful financial consulting company that services a lot of the small businesses in the area," said Hazel.

"Hmm, I see," said her mother thoughtfully. "Are he and Elliott …

"No, they're not together. Just friends," said Hazel. "He's staying with Craig because you're in town. As you can imagine, Elliott is working through many things right now. He's started a new business and is trying to build a consulting list of his own."

"It sounds overwhelming," said her mother.

"I think it is," Hazel said, not giving away the times she'd seen Elliott second-guessing himself, torn by the disappointment he'd caused his parents. She didn't want to speak for Elliott, so she kept quiet.

They walked into her office, and Hazel proudly showed her some of the calendars and organizational work she'd done with schedules and with the retail and second-hand shops.

"I'm very proud of you, Hazel," said her mother, giving her a quick hug. "These are a lot of details to handle, and you're doing a great job of it."

"Thanks. I enjoy the work, which I think is more suitable for me than teaching. Still, I help with camp for the kids and various kids' classes and enjoy that too."

They walked through the rest of the facility, watching different people and groups enjoying various activities.

When they walked out to the tennis courts, an

intermediate class for children was in session with Tracy. Hazel was delighted to see Jed and stopped outside the fence to watch him play. She pointed Jed out to her mother.

"He's a cute boy," her mother said, and waved back when Jed waved to them.

"Jed Abbott, pay attention," shouted Tracy, turning to give Hazel and her mother dirty looks.

"My! Who is that?" said her mother.

"Tracy is one of our tennis teachers," said Hazel, moving them along. But she, too, had noticed how rude Tracy was.

At the baseball field, Ross was standing by as a baseball player was at batting practice, taking pitches from another player.

Ross saw them and walked over. "Hi, Hazel. I assume this is your mother."

"Yes, meet Helena Belmont. You were talking business at the Lilac Café, or we would've stopped by your table."

"And by the time we were through with our business meeting, you were gone," explained Ross. "How are you liking our little gem of a town?" he asked her mother.

"It's lovely. Very charming. I can see why Hazel wants to stay here," her mother said, smiling.

"She's been a terrific addition to the Sports Center team," said Ross. "Are you going to bring your mother to Jake's tomorrow?"

"Yes," said Hazel. "I want her to meet everyone."

"Then you'll meet my wife and the group of friends who make this home," said Ross to her mother.

"I can't wait," she replied.

Mike approached them wearing tennis shorts and a green

shirt that complemented his eyes. Hazel couldn't help staring at how his clothes outlined his masculine body, accentuating his broad chest, narrow waist, and muscular frame.

"Hello," said Mike, coming closer. He stopped and smiled at her, and Hazel thought for a frozen moment that he might hug or kiss her to keep up appearances of dating.

"Sorry, I'm all sweaty, but it's nice to see you here," he said, grinning at Hazel.

"Thanks, we're headed home," said Hazel, hoping to forestall any conversation in front of Ross.

"We'll see you shortly," said Hazel's mother to him.

Ross raised his eyebrows but remained quiet as Hazel gave both men a wave of her hand and took hold of her mother's elbow to lead her away.

CHAPTER EIGHTEEN

While her mother relaxed on the deck, Hazel worked on getting dinner organized. Both Mike and Elliott were healthy men who enjoyed their food.

Hazel made a lemon-garlic blue cheese dressing for a tossed green salad and put together the lemon chicken casserole, which was a favorite, an easy dish to make. After sautéing the chicken breasts, she put a sauce and sliced lemons on top of them in a casserole dish. She'd complete the main course with rice and her mother's favorite steamed broccoli with a honey mustard dressing.

For dessert, Elliott was picking up something from the Lilac Lake Café. Mike had mentioned bringing a bottle of wine.

After preparing the food, Hazel set the kitchen table with floral placemats, matching napkins, wine and water glasses, and sparkling silverware. In the center of the table, she placed a single pink rose in a bud vase, one she'd picked from a rose bush outside the house. Since coming to Lilac Lake, Hazel had learned to cook, but she'd known since she was a small child that a table had to be well set. Her mother's tables were sometimes elaborate with multiple crystal wine glasses and water goblets, along with an array of silverware for every course.

Her mother came inside and inspected the table setting.

"I'm very pleased to see you following family traditions of

making each meal presentable, Hazel."

"Elliott is due any moment. Mike will be along after his last tennis class," said Hazel.

"I'll go freshen up," said her mother. "And please remind me to take a photograph of Elliot for Cassandra."

"Okay," said Hazel. She grabbed a glass of water and went out to the deck for a few quiet moments. Her mother was an easy-going houseguest, but it was still exhausting to try and keep everything running smoothly.

When Elliott arrived with a blueberry pie, Hazel was relieved to see him.

Hazel could tell from the tense look on his face that he was nervous about seeing her mother. But compared to his straitlaced parents, Hazel knew her mother would be much easier to be with.

She'd just given Elliott a kiss on the cheek when her mother walked into the kitchen.

"Why, hello, Elliott! It's wonderful to see you." Her mother gave him a warm hug.

"Hello, Ms. Belmont. It's nice to see you too," said Elliott, more at ease.

Hazel's mother smiled. "Now, before we forget, I want to get a photo of us together for your parents."

After taking several photos of Elliott with her mother, Hazel laughed. "I'm sure there are some satisfactory ones. I'll send them to both of you. How about a glass of wine?"

Looking relieved, Elliott said, "I'll open it and serve it to you. Why don't you two go out onto the deck to relax."

"Thanks," said Hazel. "As you can see, the bottle and glasses are on the counter."

Outside, Hazel took a seat in one of the four chairs that they'd pulled into a circle. She faced her mother. "Doesn't Elliott look great? And he seems so happy."

Her mother nodded. "Yes, it's still a bit of a shock to know why you two will never marry, but you seem fine with it."

"I am," Hazel said. "I've known for some time, so it isn't new to me. Besides, I like my life here and hope to stay."

Her mother gave her a thoughtful look. "But if Mike travels back and forth to Florida, is that what you want?"

Hazel held up a hand to stop her. "Please, Mom, Mike and I are just friends."

"But I've seen the way you look at one another," her mother protested.

"Hi, there," said Mike following Elliott out to the deck.

Hazel shot her mother a warning look and hoped that she wouldn't interfere with what she and Mike were doing.

Elliott handed them each a glass of wine, then handed out a bowl of mixed nuts before sitting down. He lifted his glass of wine. "Here's to family friends. Ms. Belmont, we're so pleased to have you here."

They toasted Hazel's mother, and then she gazed from Mike to Hazel, smiling sweetly. "Hopefully, I'll be back again soon. Perhaps with my husband. He, too, should probably meet everyone."

Elliott winked at Hazel, aware of how pushy her mother could sometimes be.

Hazel bit her lip. She didn't dare look at Mike.

"Tomorrow at Jake's, you'll meet even more people," said Mike, smoothing the momentary awkwardness away. "It's an interesting group."

Her mother studied Mike, and her lips curved.

Oh, no, thought Hazel. Her mother was warming up to Mike.

"Elliott, tell me about your new business," said her mother, and Hazel leaned back in her chair more relaxed.

Mike lifted her hand and gave it a squeeze.

Hazel turned to him.

"Chill," said Mike quietly, and she loved how he had picked up on her concern. For someone who was supposed to be just a friend, he was more sensitive to her feelings than the men she'd dated. She liked that about him.

The more Elliott talked about his plans, the happier he seemed. Even Hazel's mother reacted more enthusiastically as time went on.

When Hazel went into the kitchen to finish dinner, Mike followed her inside.

"Need any help?" he asked.

"You can fill the water goblets on the table," she said. "I have to steam the broccoli and toss the salad. The chicken casserole looks as if it might be done." She turned on the heat under the pan with the broccoli.

"Wow! You've got this organized," said Mike. "It smells delicious, too. I can't seem to get everything done at the same time."

"Doesn't Tracy cook?"

He shook his head. "Tracy never did much of anything around the house. She's moving out tomorrow morning, going back to Florida to be with an old boyfriend of hers. After she agreed to come to New Hampshire for the summer session at the Sports Center, I offered her a place to stay. Though it might have appeared differently, that's all it was. She was my co-worker. Nothing more than friends. I'm too busy to get seriously involved with anyone."

"Who's going to take her place at the Center?" asked Hazel.

"Ross found a guy who's willing to help us for the time being. We'll see how he works out. The Sports Center is doing well, and we're facing busier winter months."

"That's why I'm developing some new publicity ideas," said Hazel. "I'll present them to you and Ross after my mother leaves." She handed Mike the water pitcher and checked the broccoli.

While the broccoli finished cooking, Hazel got out the ingredients for a tossed salad.

"Done," said Mike, returning with the pitcher and sitting on one of the bar stools to watch her work.

A few minutes later, she handed him the salad bowl to place on the table and put together the broccoli dish her mother loved.

Hazel went to the sliding glass door to call her mother and Elliott to dinner, but stopped when she heard soft murmurs. Peering onto the deck, she saw her mother hugging Elliott and dabbing her eyes with a handkerchief.

Not wanting to intrude, she stepped back.

A moment later, she called out in a cheerful voice, "Dinner's ready!"

Her mother and Elliott appeared, smiling as if they'd resolved their issues. Hazel let out a sigh of relief. She knew how much her mother had wanted Elliott and her to marry and how hurt her mother's best friend, Cassandra, was.

The four of them sat at the table in a comfortable group. Throughout dinner, Mike regaled them with stories of some of his experiences teaching tennis to a broad range of people.

"Mike has a real following here. Everyone wants at least one training session with him," said Hazel, giving him a warm smile.

"You must have a lot of patience," Hazel's mother said to Mike. "The pro at our club chaffs a bit impatiently if people don't listen or don't seem to understand what he's saying."

"It can be frustrating at times," said Mike, "but if people are sincere about wanting to learn, I don't mind." He chuckled. "They're usually more frustrated than I am."

"How about we have coffee and dessert on the deck?" said Hazel. "It's a pleasant night."

They all carried their dishes to the kitchen sink, and then Hazel said, "Elliott and I have this, Mom. You and Mike can relax outside."

"I brought blueberry pie. Anyone want vanilla ice cream with it?" asked Elliott. "I brought that earlier."

They all decided to add ice cream, and while Hazel cut slices of pie, Elliot served a dollop of ice cream on top.

"How did things go with Mom?" Hazel asked him.

"Better than I'd hoped. She's sad that you and I won't marry, but she seems genuinely glad for me," Elliott said.

"My mother can be difficult, but she's very honest. If she said she's happy for you, then she truly is," said Hazel. "I'm glad. Our families have been close for all of our lives. I would hate for anything to come between them."

"I'm not going to spring anything too sudden onto our parents, but I've agreed to go out with Brooks Beckman. We're going to a concert in Gilford."

"Oh, that should be fun," said Hazel. She gave him a quick hug and then helped to carry desserts outside. No one wanted coffee, so she brought out glasses and the water pitcher.

When they bit into the pie, the group as one groaned with pleasure.

"This is delicious," her mother said. "No wonder the Café does so well. And, Hazel, you've done a wonderful job with dinner. I'm impressed with your cooking."

"I confess I wrote to Marianne to ask for a few of the family recipes," said Hazel. She turned to Mike. "Marianne has worked for our family for as long as I can remember. She's a tiny woman with red hair and a heart of gold who wouldn't let me or her daughter, Dolly, get away with anything growing up."

"She's been a fabulous help to me since she left her family's farm all those years ago," said her mother. "We were young mothers together, who helped each other. Dolly is a law student at LSU."

Mike gave her mother a thoughtful look and shifted uncomfortably in his seat.

Hazel knew he was comparing her past to his and sighed. He was far more accomplished than many of her spoiled friends, who merely followed in their parents' footsteps, like Elliott's parents had wanted him to do.

Hazel placed a hand on his arm.

Her mother stared at the two of them and gave them a nod of approval.

When it came time for Mike to leave, Hazel said, "I'll walk you out."

Mike said goodbye to her mother and Elliott, and as they started to walk away, he wrapped an arm around Hazel's shoulder.

"What are you doing?" whispered Hazel as they went to the front door.

"I'm playing my part," Mike said, giving her a sexy grin.

"But ...

"It's okay," said Mike, stepping outside with her. "I like that we're becoming friends. You once thought I was a playboy. I hope you now realize I'm not really like that."

She studied his earnest expression, seeing vulnerability in his green eyes.

"I know," she said, reaching up on her toes and giving him a quick kiss on his cheek. "Thanks for being a friend."

CHAPTER NINETEEN

DURING THE NIGHT, SHE'D LAIN AWAKE THINKING ABOUT Mike. Between his doing her a favor and his attachment to Jed, she'd come to understand a man far different from the one she'd thought she'd known. It was true that women fell all over themselves for his attention at the Sports Center. But while he was polite, Mike was never rude or overtly sexual with his responses. Knowing about his background made it easier to understand what he covered up with his easy-going manner—the basic insecurity of living without a family of his own.

The next morning, Hazel said goodbye to her mother, who was sitting on the deck sipping a cup of coffee, and left for her tennis match. Her mother planned to wander through town, and this evening, Hazel would take her to Jake's.

She thought about Jed. In a few weeks, she'd come to love that kind, sweet boy. She'd do anything to keep him from getting hurt.

She parked her car and went to the tennis courts, and saw both Jed and Mike ready to play.

"Hi," she said, noticing they remained seated with glum expressions. "What's up?"

Mike shot Hazel a look of concern. "Jed overheard Lisa and her husband talk about moving. I promised him I'd ask Lisa about it."

"I'll go with you," said Hazel. She placed a hand on Jed's

shoulders. "Don't worry, we won't let anything bad happen to you."

Mike stood. "Okay, time for some tennis. Jed, I want to watch you do an outstanding job with your serve."

"You serve and I'll return it," Hazel said, teasing Jed with a smile he returned. She got out her racket from the carrier and took a swing with it.

"I've got a bucket of balls for you to use," said Mike.

They walked onto the court, and time was lost as Jed and Hazel competed.

"Okay, that's enough," said Mike. "We'll stop a few minutes early, so Hazel and I can talk to Lisa."

Jed gave them a solemn nod. "Okay."

The three of them headed down the street.

Mike and Hazel waited on the porch while Jed went inside to get Lisa.

Lisa came to the door holding baby Simon. "Hi, there," she said cheerfully. "What can I do for you?"

"Jed overheard you and your husband discuss moving. I promised him we'd speak to you about it," said Mike.

"We want to make sure he'll be fine," Hazel said.

"I see," said Lisa. "At this point, it's just talk. My husband has applied for a much better job in Pennsylvania. We don't know if he'll get it."

"If you move out of state, how does that affect Jed?" Hazel asked, aware Jed was listening.

"It's something we'd have to work on," said Lisa. She, too, was aware of Jed's presence.

"So, no matter what, it would be a matter of time. Is that right? asked Hazel.

"Yes, I will keep you informed," said Lisa. "Jed, can you please go check on Harry? It's getting awfully quiet in his room."

Jed left them, and Lisa said, "If we move out of state, we may or may not be able to take Jed with us. It has to be arranged between the states. It's something I worry about."

"If necessary, would you be amenable to my becoming his foster parent?" Hazel asked, surprising herself.

"Or me," said Mike.

"You'd both have to be certified. All the information is online," said Lisa, turning as Jed approached, holding onto the toddler's hand.

"Here he is," said Jed.

Harry looked up at them and grinned.

"Jed, we'll see you tomorrow, okay?" said Mike. "We've talked with Lisa. You won't be left out of any information."

"We're here to help if you need it," said Hazel.

Jed studied their faces and then nodded with satisfaction.

"You two are the kindest couple," gushed Lisa. "We appreciate all you're doing for Jed. Isn't that right, Jed?"

He smiled and waved as Hazel and Mike prepared to leave.

As they walked away, Mike and Hazel were quiet.

Lisa had called them a couple. Hazel surprised herself by liking the idea, then told herself to be realistic. Mike had said he was too busy to think of anything like a relationship.

Finally, Hazel said, "I'm going to find out exactly what I'd have to do to become a foster parent. I believe they let single people become foster parents for children. I'll check on it. The cabin has plenty of room for Jed."

Mike gave her a steady look. "Let me know what we have to do. I'll sign up for any classes and do whatever it takes. We can't let Jed go into another foster home. Even an acceptable one. He needs stability."

Hazel heard the determination in Mike's voice and knew he was remembering his childhood.

As soon as Hazel went to her office, she looked up information online.

She learned that it typically takes sixty days or more to become a licensed foster care provider. There's no minimum age. A home study is required, and a 21-hour course completed. Background checks and medical records are required.

Hazel sat back in her chair and let out a long sigh. There was so much to think about. She wouldn't mention this idea of hers to anyone else but Mike. It would be their secret until or if it became time to act.

Following another busy day, Hazel drove home. She was going to take her mother to Jake's tonight, and they had enough time before then to sit with a glass of wine. Tomorrow, her mother was leaving for home. Hazel wanted to make sure her mother was satisfied with her short visit.

Later, after an easy discussion between the two of them, they got ready to go to Jake's.

On the way downtown, Hazel explained that those who were free met for drinks and dinner once or twice a week and caught up with the news.

"It's an interesting group of people who are very active in town with their businesses and influence," said Hazel.

"Like having Ross Roberts so much a part of the town?" asked her mother.

"Exactly. It was helpful to have names like Ross Roberts and Mike Dawson behind the Sports Center for local and state support. But shopkeepers and small business owners all play a part. And it is these friends who make such a difference in the success of the town."

"It's so nice that people your age can play a part in maintaining the quality of life in this community," said her mother. "I hope that lovely woman who owns the Wild Flower Boutique will be there."

"That's Poppy Browning."

They parked behind the bar and walked around to the front entrance.

As they entered, Hazel saw that several people were already sitting at the tables in the back, reserved for the locals.

Smiling, she waved and led her mother over to them.

Still standing, Hazel introduced her mother and asked everyone there to introduce themselves, which they did, going around the tables in a big circle.

Her mother chuckled. "It's lovely to meet y'all. Please forgive me if I don't remember all of your names."

Hazel chose to sit in the empty chair next to Mike, with her mother seated on her other side.

From across the table, Melissa said, "Mike was just telling us that Tracy moved back to Florida and someone else will be coming to Lilac Lake to replace her."

"I did find her a bit abrasive," said Sarah, sitting beside Aaron. "Maybe it's a good thing."

"Ross and I were doing her a favor by having her join the

staff for the summer," said Mike.

"We had no idea that she was unwilling to put in much effort," said Ross. "But then, our business has grown at an outstanding rate due to our administrator." He grinned at Hazel.

"I knew she'd do a fantastic job," said Misty. "She'll be sorely missed at school this year."

Their waitress came to the table with drinks and food for some of the others, and Hazel and her mother ordered.

Brad began talking about Collister Construction and The Meadows, the upscale housing development outside of town. "We're having our first family move out of the neighborhood. They just notified us of their intention to do so because he's got a new job on the West Coast."

"So, it's for sale?" asked Mike.

"It's not on the market yet, but it will be," said Brad.

"Can I take a look at it?" Mike said. "We're going to move our new tennis pro into the condo I'm renting, and I think it's time for me to have something more permanent here. And with Ross and Melissa in the neighborhood, it kind of makes sense for me to be there too."

Brad grinned. "That would be great." He looked over to Aaron for his approval, and Aaron gave his silent agreement.

"Okay, I'll call you tomorrow to set up a time," said Mike. He turned to Hazel. "Maybe you'll look at it with me. I need a woman's opinion."

"Sure," she said. "I love looking at real estate."

Hazel could feel her mother beaming at them without even looking at her. But she remained quiet. Not everyone knew what fake dating scheme she and Mike had cooked up.

The waitress arrived, and to Hazel's relief, her mother's attention became focused on the fish dinner she'd ordered.

Other locals came and went, giving her mother a very complete introduction to Hazel's group of friends.

When it came time for them to leave, Mike said, "I'll walk you out."

They made their way to the door and stepped outside.

Her mother stood and gazed around. "I love all the sparkly lights. Honestly, this is such a charming town."

"I know you're leaving tomorrow morning, but I wanted to say how nice it was to meet you," said Mike politely. He held out his hand, and Hazel's mother took it, gazing into his face.

"And it was lovely to meet you, Mike. I'm sure I'll be seeing more of you. I see how you and Hazel are with one another."

Mike glanced at Hazel and winked.

Hazel couldn't help the wave of happiness that filled her, and then chided herself for thinking that his reaction was reality. He was simply playing his part well. So well that she was charmed by him.

CHAPTER TWENTY

Driving her mother to the airport outside Portsmouth, Hazel had mixed feelings. The visit had gone better than expected. But with her mother gone, where did that leave her and Mike? Especially worrisome was the idea that her mother wanted to return to New Hampshire so her father could meet and judge Mike for himself.

Hazel told herself to stick with the "just dating idea" so it wouldn't be so disappointing if she and Mike "broke up."

Another cause of concern was her idea of going ahead and becoming certified to become a foster parent in New Hampshire if the need ever became real with Jed.

"You're very quiet," said her mother. "Is everything all right?"

"I'm sad to see you go," said Hazel. "But I'm glad your life is so full at home. I hope you have a much better grasp of why Elliott wants to stay here. I'm excited that he's finally becoming himself, not hiding who he is from parents who've always expected too much of him."

"I agree. Elliott and I had a long talk. I've loved him since he was a child, and I want him to be happy. I'm sure Cassandra will understand better after we have a chance to talk."

"That'll be a big help to Elliott. He's never wanted to disappoint them," said Hazel.

She pulled into a parking spot and helped her mother inside the terminal.

They stood staring at one another, and then her mother said, "I hate goodbyes." She wrapped her arms around Hazel and kissed her. "See you another time."

Hazel murmured, "Love you," and thought of Jed and others like him who might never have been as lucky to have such a loving mother.

On her way back to town, she got a call from Mike.

"I'm on my way to The Meadows to look at the house Brad was talking about last night. Are you able to join me? I was serious when I said I needed a woman's perspective on it. I want to see if it could be a suitable place for Jed if I should ever need to foster him."

"I'm sure it will be fine for that, but I'm curious to see the house," said Hazel. "I promise to be truthful." She chuckled. "I hope you know I don't normally deceive people. But in my mother's case, I knew what would happen if I didn't come up with something to keep her at bay."

"Your mother is a very nice woman who wants the best for her daughter," said Mike. "I admire her."

"She really liked you," said Hazel.

"Your mother was very pleasant to me, but make no mistake, I realize we're from very different backgrounds. Your family has a housekeeper, belongs to a country club, and has always had a privileged life."

"But that's not me or *my* life," countered Hazel, upset by the thought of Mike thinking he wasn't good enough for her. He was a lot more thoughtful than most of the so-called suitable men who came from her background.

"Well, it's a moot choice. We did a satisfying job

convincing your mother she didn't need to put so much pressure on you. What did she think of the idea of fostering Jed?"

"I haven't mentioned it," said Hazel. "I need to get the training and applications done before discussing it with her. But if it happens, that's my decision. Not hers."

She ended the call with Mike and continued driving to The Meadows, lost in thought. If she were totally honest with herself, she'd admit that she was falling for Mike. Hard. And she had no idea what to do about it.

The sign for The Meadows appeared. Hazel drove into the development and over to the reception building. Mike saw her, got out of his car, and waited for her to join him.

Inside the office, Mike talked to Melanie Perkins from Lake Realty, who was handling sales for the development. Melanie was a middle-aged woman with bright red hair who kept track of everyone in town. If you had nothing to hide, you had nothing to fear.

Now, she rose from behind her desk and hurried over to greet them with handshakes and quizzical looks. "Who do we have here? Are you Mike Dawson?"

"Yes," said Mike. "And this is my friend, Hazel Belmont. I'm the tennis pro at the Sports Center, and Hazel is the administrator there."

"Aw, yes. I've heard such positive things about the Sports Center. I've been meaning to apply for a swim membership," said Melanie.

"Now is a wise time to do it," said Hazel. "We're filling those memberships quickly."

Melanie looked at her and smiled. "An enthusiastic

administrator. Too bad you're not interested in real estate."

Hazel laughed. "I've got my hands full with the job I have."

"Please sit, and I'll tell you about the house you'll see," said Melanie. "It's a great opportunity for a couple who wants to grow their family. It has a lot of flexibility. There are four bedrooms, a small office, a small dining room, and a family great room that opens into the kitchen. Depending on what you want, you could use the dining room for a formal living room, turn the kitchen into a larger dining area, and so on. The small office could be turned into a nursery because it's not far from the master suite."

"It all sounds fine," said Mike.

"The fenced backyard is bigger than some others who chose to keep theirs natural with wooded lots," said Melanie.

"I'm anxious to see it," said Hazel.

Melanie stood. "Here are the keys. I've arranged for the family living there to be absent."

Mike held the door for Hazel and then followed her outside.

"It's bigger than I need right now, but as I told the gang last night, I'm ready to make Lilac Lake my permanent home," said Mike.

"I like the idea that it's flexible. Let's see for ourselves," said Hazel.

They walked down the road of large homes built on sizeable lots. The fifth house on the left was a contemporary-style home stained a warm brown. It had lots of glass windows that gave an openness to the house.

The front door was painted an evergreen color and held a

colorful floral wreath. Beside the door sat a pot of red geraniums.

Hazel followed Mike onto the porch and waited while he unlocked the door.

Stepping inside, the entryway led to a closet on one side and a powder room on the other side. The open space beyond the entry held a family room with a stone fireplace to the right and a dining room to the left. The back of the house beyond the family room contained a kitchen and a laundry room. The master bedroom suite was off to the left.

As Hazel and Mike walked through the house, Hazel commented on the quality of the finishing touches. Though the owners had chosen different colors in different bedrooms, Hazel liked the idea of pale-gray paint on the walls throughout the main rooms. She could see herself living here. Especially with Mike. Not that she'd ever say so.

"The master bath has everything," said Mike, studying the oversized shower and separate spa tub.

"I love the private deck off the bedroom," said Hazel. "A marvelous place to have coffee in the morning."

"Let's look upstairs," said Mike.

They climbed the stairs and found a large bedroom with its ensuite bathroom, and another two bedrooms with a Jack-and-Jill bathroom between them. The wide landing at the top of the stairs was presently serving as a toy room.

"What kid wouldn't love a house like this?" said Mike. "What do you think? Money is not a problem. I still get funds from companies that sponsored me when I played tennis nationally, and for being part of several advertising campaigns for them and others. I've invested all the money and used some dividends to participate in the Sports Center ownership."

"I think it would be a wise investment if you could get it for a fair price. It's a beautiful home. And we both know The Meadows is the premier housing development in the area. Even the ex-governor and his wife live here."

They went downstairs for another look around.

As Hazel stood in the kitchen gazing out at the screened porch and beyond it to the woods, Mike came up behind her.

She turned and found herself in his arms.

Heart pounding, she gazed up at his face.

Seeing the hunger in his eyes, she put her arms around him and laid her head on his chest. She could hear the pounding of his heart and sighed with contentment.

He lifted her chin and gazed at her with a tender expression. "I'm going to fight for you, Hazel. I want you in my life. You're the best person I know. I don't care what anyone thinks about me except you. I want to prove to you that I can make you truly happy. I fell for you for real the first time I saw you with Jed."

Mike lowered his lips to hers.

Feelings she didn't know she had exploded in a burst of desire. She'd imagined what his lips might feel and taste like, but she was unprepared for the shock of need that went through her.

When they pulled apart, she gazed at him in a daze.

"Wow," he murmured, caressing her face in his broad hands.

She smiled at him. "Yeah, wow."

He laughed. "Okay, let's begin this journey of ours.

Hopefully, it will be everything we both want."

Hazel felt tears spring to her eyes. She felt lucky to have discovered Mike's true nature. He was an exceptional man who wanted to be loved and was willing to return it to her and show it to a little boy named Jed.

CHAPTER TWENTY-ONE

OVER THE NEXT SEVERAL DAYS, MIKE WORKED WITH Melanie to devise a deal to buy the house. Because he was flexible about putting off the purchase date, they agreed to a very fair price, making all parties satisfied.

The new tennis pro, Paco Sanchez, was elated to be in town working at the Sports Center. His girlfriend, Mallory Warren, was given the job of running the camps for kids, something Tracy was supposed to have done.

Hazel worked with Mallory, helping her to organize schedules and come up with extra games and activities for the students.

One morning, Ross stopped in Hazel's office. "How are things going with Mallory?"

"Good. She's eager to help and is great with the kids. Much more committed and positive than Tracy. The kids love her."

"I'm glad to hear that." He paused. "So, you and Mike are together. He seems very happy about it."

"We're seeing how a relationship might go," Hazel said primly, unwilling to seem overly confident. Thoughts of their lovemaking last night made her cheeks blush and heat roar through her. Mike was an exciting lover, passionate and generous.

Ross beamed at her. "I think the two of you are great together. It's about time Mike found some true happiness."

After he left the office, Hazel sat quietly thinking of Mike. They'd talked for hours about their thoughts for the future, what it might mean to have a foster child, and that fostering meant the children were in your life forever.

Mike couldn't get over the fact that Hazel was excited about the possibility of fostering Jed, or if that didn't work out, fostering another child at a later date.

"You're a very special woman," he told her one night as they curled up on the couch to watch TV together. "I'm sorry I didn't make a favorable impression on you when you first came to town."

"You had women of all ages falling over you. I thought you liked that kind of attention," Hazel said. "Now, I know better. It's just part of your job."

"My job now is to make you happy," teased Mike.

She laughed. "It's a two-way street. Staying here with me until the house is ready will be a big test of that."

"Thanks for letting me turn the condo over to Paco and Mallory," he said. "That gives them an easy start. I've told them about coming to Jake's this Saturday."

"I hope they stay and become part of the town. Everyone likes them and the way they work at their jobs. They're a good addition to the group."

"I should've known better than to agree to hire Tracy," Mike said.

Saturday evening, Hazel and Mike decided to meet up at Jake's rather than go together. Hazel was glad they had. Her girlfriends gathered around her and quizzed her on what had happened between Mike and her and when their relationship had begun for real.

Hazel managed to get most of the information out before Mike showed up.

When Mike greeted her with a kiss, she heard a couple of her friends sigh. Theirs was a sweet story—pretending to be together and then making it happen.

Soon, Elliott and Brooks Beckman arrived, and everyone's attention turned to them.

When Paco and Mallory showed up, both Ross and Mike made sure they were introduced to everyone.

Sitting there, chatting and eating with the others, Hazel liked the feeling of being included. Her thoughts drifted to Jed. She hoped, whether he went with Lisa and her family or ended up here in Lilac Lake, that he'd have this same sense of belonging.

Later, when people started to leave, Mike turned to her. "Ready to go home?"

She drew in a breath, caught off guard by how easily those words came to Mike and what they meant to both of them.

At home, she removed her clothes, put them in a hamper, and slid on the oversized T-shirt she wore to bed. In the bathroom, she moved aside some of Mike's things sitting on the countertop and brushed her teeth.

When she returned to the bedroom, she saw Mike's dirty clothes tossed against the hamper and frowned.

"What?" asked Mike.

"Please pick up your clothes and put them inside the hamper? I don't like a mess."

"Sorry," Mike said. "Guess it will take a while to get used

to living together."

"Might as well deal with it now," said Hazel. She'd just read an article about the pitfalls of living with someone, and she knew they'd both have to make compromises.

Mike brought up the issue of bras drying in the shower after handwashing.

She mentioned that he put dishes in the kitchen sink, but not the dishwasher.

The back and forth ended with a lot of laughter over how the toilet paper rolls should be hung.

Still laughing, Mike put his arms around Hazel and nuzzled her neck. "We can do this."

"Oh, yes," said Hazel. She turned and snuggled up against him. "We'll make this work."

The next morning, they got up together and hurried over to the tennis courts to meet Jed.

Since they'd talked to Lisa about moving, they'd heard nothing.

"Hi," said Hazel, giving Jed a big smile. "Ready to play?"

"Yep. Today I'm going to beat you," Jed told her.

'You're both improving," said Mike. "Let's work on backhands today."

While Mike watched, giving them pointers, Hazel played a few games with Jed until it was time for the lesson to be over.

"You're so talented," Hazel said to Jed, wiping the sweat off her face with a towel. She handed Jed a bottle of water and took one for herself before sitting on the bench outside the court.

Jed sat beside her. "I want to be a tennis pro like Mike."

"You've got the talent for it," said Mike. "But it takes lots and lots of practice."

"Lisa told me that," said Jed.

"Have you heard anything more about moving?" asked Hazel.

Jed shook his head. "Lisa said not to worry about it. But I don't want to leave Lilac Lake. It's the best home I've ever had."

Hazel and Mike exchanged worried glances.

"Just remember, we're here to help any way we can," said Hazel, careful not to promise too much. But today she'd follow through to see when she and Mike could sign up for the training course.

Two nights later, Hazel sat in on a foster parent training class with Mike. Listening to some of the stories and all that would be required of her, Hazel was feeling overwhelmed until she remembered that all parents with a new baby probably felt the same.

Mike wrote down notes on a paper pad while she underlined things in the printed handouts they'd been given. It pleased her that both of them wanted to get it right.

When the course ended, the instructor waved them over. "I heard what you said about wanting to help out a child in our system whose foster parents might be moving out of state. It doesn't always have to be a difficult process to transfer a child, but often it takes time, and sometimes it doesn't work out. I'm confused, though. Which one of you wants the child?"

"I do," said Mike and Hazel together.

The instructor studied them. "Single foster parents are

allowed, but you'd do much better to be living together, working as a team, married even, if it comes to an in-state decision. Just a thought."

Hazel turned to face Mike.

"We're just beginning our relationship," he told the instructor. He glanced at Hazel. "But it's something to think about."

As they left the building, both Hazel and Mike were silent.

"I don't want to be pushed into anything," said Hazel.

"Me either," Mike said. 'I like living together, though."

"Let's see how things unfold," said Hazel. "It's working so far, but let's not jump ahead of ourselves."

"I agree," said Mike. "I'm relieved to hear you say that."

Hazel remembered how Mike had said he'd fight for her. She hoped they weren't empty words.

CHAPTER TWENTY-TWO

THE MID-SUMMER TENNIS TOURNAMENTS AT THE SPORTS Center were something Hazel had worked hard on. For all ages, the matches ran from early morning to evening for two days. She was especially excited about the kids' tournaments on day one. There were three. One for ten to twelve-year-olds, one for kids thirteen to sixteen, and lastly, one for seventeen to twenty.

Both Hazel and Mike were looking forward to seeing Jed's match. He'd wanted to play against older kids, but Mike thought it was best if he competed with kids more his age in the first group.

On this late July morning, Hazel stood watching Jed prepare on one side of the court, facing a twelve-year-old who was talented for his age.

Once play began, it was evident how much Jed wanted to win with the way he moved and swung his racket, putting his natural talents and strength to work.

In one instance, a rally between the boys went on and on with each player determined to win the point.

When a soft shot dropped on Jed's side of the net, Jed shot forward to get it and tripped. In his eagerness to win the point, he'd stretched too far and lost his balance. He stumbled, twisting his ankle, and fell to the ground with a shriek of pain. His racket clattered to the hard surface beside him.

Hazel and Mike rushed onto the court.

"Ow!" Jed held onto his ankle as tears rolled down his cheeks.

"Be careful. Don't move him," said Hazel, kneeling beside Jed and holding onto his hand.

Mike called the EMTs.

Hazel swept a hand across Jed's brow, looked into his eyes, and said, "Lie still. We're getting help for you."

Outside the fence, spectators gathered, trying to get a look at the situation.

The boy Jed had been playing against looked on from the circle of concerned people who'd formed around Jed. "I'm sorry."

Hazel looked at him and shook her head. "It's not your fault. It was an accident. That's all."

Mike returned to them, and shortly afterward, the EMTs arrived on the scene.

After checking Jed over carefully, one of the men said, "It looks like a badly sprained ankle. But we need to make sure. We can take him over to the Emergency Clinic to be checked out."

"We have to wait for his foster mother to approve," said Hazel, still holding onto Jed's hand. "She's on her way."

She looked up as Mike and Lisa hurried toward them.

"Oh, Jed! I'm here," Lisa said, taking hold of Jed's free hand and turning to the EMTs. "How bad is he hurt?"

"We think it's a badly sprained ankle," said one of the EMT's, giving her more details. "We can take him to the clinic here in Lilac Lake, and you can ride with him."

"Okay," said Lisa. "I'll go with him."

Jed whimpered and clung to Hazel's hand.

"Where are the other children? Do you need me to help?" Hazel asked her.

"They're okay. My neighbor is with them," said Lisa. "But maybe Jed would like you to come to the clinic too."

Jed nodded emphatically.

The EMTs put Jed on a stretcher and carried him over to the ambulance.

Lisa and Hazel climbed into the vehicle beside him.

"Pretty exciting to get a ride in an ambulance," said Lisa, smiling gently at Jed.

His lips quivered and he turned to Hazel. "When can I play tennis again?"

"We'll see," Hazel said. She'd heard bad sprains could be more challenging to deal with than a bone break. Either way, it would be some time before Jed could play again.

They arrived at the Emergency Clinic that Crystal's husband, Dr. Emmett Chambers, had created in addition to handling his practice. The EMTs explained what they'd found to a nurse, and Jed was placed on a bed in an examination room.

While Lisa talked to the receptionist, Hazel stood by Jed as Dr. Chambers came into the room to examine him.

Hazel was impressed by the gentle way her friend, Emmett, talked to Jed as he examined him.

"We'll take an X-ray of the ankle to clarify the injury and then we'll see what we can do about helping with the pain. Does that sound okay?" he asked Jed, speaking to Lisa and Hazel as well.

Jed was quiet as a nurse lifted him into a wheelchair and

rolled him away.

"Good luck," Hazel said to him.

"It'll be fine," said Lisa, giving Jed a pat on the back.

After they left, Hazel waited in the exam room with Lisa.

Lisa's eyes filled as she turned to Hazel. "Thank you for staying with Jed and me. I see how he's bonded with you. It's a good thing because my husband and I might not be able to make the move with him. The case worker says there could be some restrictions on taking him out of state." She sniffed. "We love that boy and want to take him with us. But there might be a period of time before that can happen. I'm hoping you would be willing to help us while we work on the issue."

"I would do anything to help Jed. Mike, too," said Hazel.

The conversation stopped when Jed was rolled back into the room by the doctor.

"Well, how's my boy?" asked Lisa, coming to Jed's side and holding his hand.

"Nothing is broken, but he's had a bad sprain," said Emmett. "I've wrapped the ankle with an elastic bandage to wear until the swelling has gone down. Then we'll transition him into a soft boot to give the ankle stability. He tells me he doesn't need crutches, that he'll hop on his other foot until he has a boot."

"I told the doctor I want to play tennis," said Jed.

Hazel exchanged glances with the other two adults in the room and kept quiet.

"We're going to help you heal as quickly as you can," Emmett said to Jed. "I'm giving your mother a topical NSAID to put on your ankle to help with the pain. You're to keep your foot elevated and still. And you'll need to ice it for 15 minutes three or four times a day."

Jed frowned and looked down at his bandaged foot.

Emmett patted him on the back. "You're young and healthy. The closer attention you pay to my instructions, the faster you'll heal. I'll see you back here in a week."

After he left, Jed looked at Lisa and Hazel with a gloomy expression. "What am I going to do all day?"

"For once, you can sit and watch television," said Lisa.

"I'll bring you some games or something to keep you occupied," said Hazel. "Is that all right, Lisa?"

"Yes," said Lisa. "That would be very kind."

When the three of them walked into the waiting room, Mike stood up from his seat on the couch and walked over to Jed sitting in a wheelchair. "How's the tennis star?"

"I can't play for a while," said Jed, pouting.

"But the doctor says he's young and healthy and should heal quickly," Hazel said.

"Sounds like a plan," said Mike to Jed before turning to Lisa. "I can give you a ride home anytime you're ready."

"Thanks so much, I'm not sure what I'd do without your help."

Crystal, who helped Emmett in the office regularly, came from behind the reception desk. "I'll email you the necessary paperwork so you can take care of it, Lisa. In the meantime, let us know if any problems come up. I understand Jed didn't want crutches and will do well holding on to someone and hopping. If that changes, let us know."

"Thank you," said Lisa. "Now we need to get this boy home."

Mike carried Jed to his car and placed him in the

backseat. Lisa climbed in beside him, while Hazel sat in the passenger seat.

After sliding behind the wheel, Mike drove to Lisa's house.

"Please wait here with Jed," said Lisa as they pulled into the driveway. "Let me go inside and make sure everything is ready for him. He'll be staying on the couch for the next week, and I want to make sure we've got room for him there."

After Lisa dashed into the house, Jed began to cry. "I don't want to stay home on the couch. I want to play tennis. If I don't play tennis, you'll forget me."

Hazel turned in her seat to face him, sitting in the back. "We're very special friends. And friends don't forget friends when they can't be together. They save up their stories to share for times when they can be." She knew those very words might be important in the future when the time came for Jed to move away.

"I'll try to come up with some exercises for you to do to keep you ready to return to the courts," said Mike.

"We'll check on you. In fact, I have an idea of how we can," said Hazel, hoping she wasn't overstepping her role as a friend.

Lisa appeared on the front porch and waved them inside.

Mike and Hazel got out of the car, and while Mike lifted Jed into his arms, Hazel hurried up to the porch to see if she could help Lisa.

"Thanks," said Lisa. "Would you check on Harry? I'd appreciate it. He's a very busy toddler. Baby Simon is napping.

Hazel walked inside and saw Janis Tolland, the nurse who lived next door, packing up her things and getting ready to leave.

"Hello," said Hazel. "I'm so glad to see you. You're such a sweet neighbor."

"I'm always glad I can lend a hand," said Janis. "It sounds like Jed has some couch time coming. I'll help Lisa whenever I can."

They turned as Mike carried Jed inside and placed him on the couch.

He smiled up at Janis, and then Lisa said, "I think we're all set here. Jed needs to rest."

Harry toddled over to Jed. "You sick?"

"My ankle is," said Jed, squealing when the toddler threw himself on Jed for a hug.

Hazel used that moment to privately ask Lisa's opinion about the ideas she had to keep Jed occupied.

Lisa listened and said, "That would be wonderful. He's a lucky boy."

"Time to go," said Mike. He patted Jed on the back. "Hope you feel better, bud. Get lots of rest."

"Yes," said Hazel, hugging Jed. "Do as the doctor said, so you can heal faster."

Jed nodded solemnly, his eyes swimming with tears.

Outside, Hazel let out a long sigh. "Let's go somewhere where we can talk."

"I know the perfect place," said Mike. "The gang at Jake's was talking about it last time we were there."

Remembering, Hazel smiled. "I know where you mean. Let's go."

Mike drove into the center of town and over a couple of

blocks from Main Street to the park that David Graham and his family had created in his sister's memory.

"This is so pretty," said Hazel, gazing at the colorful, well-maintained flower beds lining the lot. "An oasis of peace."

Mike took hold of her hand, and they walked down the wide flagstone path to a wooden bench in the far corner.

Once they were seated, Hazel said, "I had a talk with Lisa at the Emergency Center while Jed had X-rays done. She and her husband want Jed to accompany them out of state, but there may be some difficulties they have to overcome. During that time, they might need us to help them. I didn't tell her we'd both already started the process of becoming foster parents. But I thought we should inform the authorities if we need to take Jed on for a while."

"So, we'd be his temporary foster parents while they get the paperwork sorted and approved before he could go to Pennsylvania with them?" said Mike.

"That might be the case. It's obvious that Jed is happy with them, and they love him. We don't want to interfere with that."

"I'd want to be sure Jed is okay with it," said Mike. "His moving with his family wouldn't necessarily mean he can't come and stay with us for summer tennis camps. That might be one way for him to have the best of both worlds."

"We can help him have that," said Hazel. "And maybe this is the best way to see how we want to move forward together without the added pressure of suddenly having a ten-year-old child."

Mike wrapped an arm around her shoulder and pulled her close. "It might be smart to go ahead and have home studies done on both of our houses so the proper people have an idea of how it could all work out now and, possibly, in the future."

Mike was right. Neither of them wanted to be forced into a permanent relationship before they were ready. "In the meantime, I have some ideas about making this next week a little easier for Jed. Lisa has already approved."

Mike laughed when she told him. "No kid is going to dislike that."

"We'd better get back to the Sports Center," said Hazel. "I have to see about a proper accident report being filed, and I believe you have a class."

"Tonight, I want to take you to Chica's for dinner."

"Sounds delicious," said Hazel. "I love their Mexican food, and their margaritas are the best."

Mike studied her and then kissed her, gently at first and then with more passion.

When they finally broke apart, Hazel gazed at him, knowing she'd found the man she'd waited for all her life.

CHAPTER TWENTY-THREE

THE NEXT DAY HAZEL DELIVERED A GIFT TO JED. "LISA and I talked about it and agreed you could have this to keep you busy while you lie on the couch. But you must follow her rules about its use."

Jed looked up at the two women standing together and opened the package. "For me? Really?"

"Yes," said Lisa. "But as Hazel said, there will be rules about using it."

Jed clasped the cell phone in his hands. "I've never had something like this. Thank you, Hazel."

"It's from Mike too. And he said to tell you that in a couple of days when you're feeling better, he'll come get you and take you to the Sports Center to watch some tennis matches."

"That'd be super," said Jed, smiling at her and then the phone. "This week won't be so bad."

"I'll help you get the phone set up," said Lisa. "I'll put my name and number in as well as Hazel's and Mike's. You'll be restricted from playing some of the games, but there will still be plenty of fun for you."

Hazel gave Jed a quick hug. "I've got to go back to work. Have a fun time with your phone."

Lisa walked Hazel to the door. "How can I ever thank you enough? That gift is as much help to me as it is for him."

"We thought it might be used if any future separations take place," said Hazel. "I haven't told you, but Mike and I are applying to become foster parents. That might make it easier for us to help you out during your move if it becomes necessary."

Lisa clapped her hands together. "How wonderful!" She studied Hazel. "I have to ask, why are you and Mike being so kind to Jed and me and my family?"

"I fell in love with Jed very quickly. And when I learned about his home situation and being fostered, I wanted to do everything possible to help. Mike was a foster child, himself. Though his experience was far different from Jed's life with you, he likes being supportive, too."

"I've said it before, and I'll say it again, you two are a kind, wonderful couple," said Lisa.

"Thanks. We're only recently decided to be in a relationship, but it's gratifying to hear your words," said Hazel.

"I'll let you know how the week goes," said Lisa.

"We'll call before Mike offers to pick up Jed," Hazel responded. "See you later."

The next few days were busy filling out forms, having medical exams, and attending more training classes for foster care certification. The only thing left to do was to arrange for a home inspection.

A week later, Hazel and Mike stood at the entrance to her guest room, giving it a thorough inspection. She'd been advised by Lisa to make the room look as if it were ready for a young boy.

They'd ordered and hung three big posters on the wall. One of Novak Djokovic, and two colorful generic ones with unnamed tennis players.

"This is a beautiful home. There's no need to be nervous about it," said Mike. "And Jed or any other child interested in tennis would love this room."

Hazel looked at the queen-sized bed, the bureau, and the bedside table in matching cherry wood. "Right now, it's pretty plain, but a child, like Jed, will quickly change that."

She turned to Mike. "We know that we might have Jed for a short time while Lisa and her husband arrange for him to move with them. Are you going to be ready to have him forever if they can't do it?"

"It'll be easier if we have him for a short time, but I won't let that boy go to another foster home where he might not receive the care Lisa and her husband have given him," said Mike. "The thought brings back a whole lot of bad memories."

"Okay, we'll leave it up to fate, and no matter what happens with us, we'll work together to help Jed."

"What do you mean no matter what happens with us?" asked Mike frowning. "Are you having second thoughts about our being together?"

"Not at all. I just want to be sure it's what you want," said Hazel. Everything seemed backward. They'd agreed to raise a child together, but they weren't even engaged. She needed assurance that she hadn't let her heart lead her to a major disappointment.

Mike cupped his hands around her face and gave her a steady look. "I love you, Hazel. I was hooked when we first met. But I knew what kind of family you came from and our differences. Would you have even listened to me back then?"

Hazel knew she had to be truthful. "No. That was before

I knew what kind of man you are. Now, I know better."

"Are you willing to take a chance on making us and this commitment to help Jed work?"

"Yes, Mike. I love you, too." Her lips quivered. "I really do."

Mike's cheeks flushed, and his eyes moistened. Then, his kisses told her all over again how much he loved her.

When they met with the instructor the following week, Mike and Hazel were told they passed the house inspection with flying colors. "Any child that would be staying with you would be very lucky indeed."

"Thanks," said Hazel. "Anything else?"

"For the moment, we're waiting for the paperwork from both of you to be processed. You might want to think about the fact that you both work. How will you arrange to be with a child if you're not at home?"

"I've lined up a reliable babysitter," said Hazel. "She's a delightful woman who's worked for a friend of mine and lives at The Woodlands. But during the summer months, when a child is not in school, I'll work out a schedule with Mike. If we have Jed, he'll get to spend even more time at the Sports Center."

"And if you don't get Jed?" the instructor asked.

"We'll cross that bridge when we come to it," said Mike.

Hazel knew neither of them was ready to consider that.

The instructor studied them. "Yours is an unusual situation on a personal level. I understand that. If things don't work out now for fostering, you're the kind of parents we're always looking for. Perhaps after your relationship is stabilized."

Hazel and Mike exchanged glances.

Hazel sensed Mike's reluctance to feel pushed, and she understood. Between them, they knew how they felt about one another. Surely, the timing for something more serious should be their own.

Over the next weeks, as Jed healed, Hazel and Mike grew even closer.

When Hazel's mother suggested that she and Hazel's father wanted to visit Lilac Lake to see both Hazel and Mike, she readily agreed. She knew Mike well enough to know nothing would move their relationship forward without a meeting between the two men closest to her.

"When would you like to come?" Hazel asked her mother.

"Dad and I looked over our social obligations, and as a matter of fact, we'd like to come next Monday. We'll be able to stay for just four days. We'll fly into Boston and drive up from there, so you won't have to pick us up. I know how busy you are."

"I'm happy to have the chance to see you again and to show Dad around the town," said Hazel.

"Your father wants to meet Mike," said her mother. "We were wondering if we could sign up to play pickleball for a game or two. That will be a way to show Dad how special the Sports Center is."

"I agree. I'll arrange something for you both," said Hazel.

"Your father also wants to look into fishing in the area. If he doesn't get the chance to do that this time, he'll have all the information for future visits. I fell in love with Lilac Lake and love having the opportunity to visit you."

"Okay, can't wait to see you both," said Hazel, realizing this was a big step toward the future.

When Mike heard the news, he said, "It'll be nice to have more time with your mother and to meet your father. After all, you're their only child."

"Growing up, I wished for a sibling, but that couldn't happen," said Hazel. "Maybe that's why I'm eager to help other children. The more the merrier, thing."

"Really? You know what they say, 'practice makes perfect', said Mike, drawing her into his lap as they sat on the deck.

She leaned against him, loving the feel of his arms around her. For someone who grew up without a lot of love, he luxuriated in it now. She'd never realized that about him before. But it made sense. It was one of the things about him that she admired.

"I suppose we'll have to tell them about our being certified for foster care," she said.

"Yes, it's important. Even though we might not need it for Jed, we'll have that for the future when we might be in a better position to do it."

"Of course, I want children of my own too."

"Yes, the more than merrier thing," grinned Mike, and they laughed together.

The day her parents were due to arrive, Hazel freshened the guest room, leaving the tennis posters on the wall. She put bottles of water in their room and filled a vase with fresh flowers from Petals, the florist downtown.

She wiped down the kitchen and made sure the deck was

swept and the furniture was ready for guests. She loved spending time on the deck, but sometimes the wind-ridden debris that ended up on it was a nuisance.

During a break, her parents called from the airport and gave her an estimate of when they'd arrive.

Mike arranged to come to the house to be able to greet them with Hazel as a couple, something Hazel thought was important.

Later, they were outside checking over some rhododendron bushes in the front of the house when her parents' rental car appeared.

She turned and faced them with happiness. Ever since her mother's earlier visit, Hazel felt closer to her, more like friends than mother and daughter. And as always, just seeing her father filled her with joyful knowledge that she'd always be Daddy's little girl.

Hazel waited beside Mike for her parents to get out of the car. Her mother kissed her hello and then gave Mike a quick hug.

Her father threw his arms around her, keeping an eye on Mike before kissing her on the cheek. After he released Hazel, he held out his hand. "So, you're the tennis pro. Hi, Mike, I'm Raymond Belmont. Nice to meet you."

"Mike Dawson," he said, shaking hands with him. "Let me help you with the luggage."

Her mother grabbed her purse from the car, and while the men unloaded the luggage, Hazel and her mother went inside.

"You and Dad will be staying in the guest room. I'll explain about the posters later."

While her mother freshened up and the luggage was

brought in, Hazel took out the fruit and vegetable platter she'd ordered from the Café and placed it on a table outside. It was late enough in the day to start cocktails or simply have iced tea, sweetened the way her parents liked.

Her parents opted to have a glass of wine, so Mike opened a bottle of a light rosé perfect for the afternoon.

Her father looked around at the woods and beyond them to the river. "Does the river have fish?"

"I don't know if it's a good fishing river or not," said Hazel. "But there are plenty of places to go. Mom said you wanted to find out information about it."

"Yes, I think that might be a great way to relax," her father said. He turned to Mike. "I thought that's something we might want to do together."

Mike's look of pleasure was touching. "Yes, we can see what's out there. Some of the guys in town fish and hunt."

"I told Hazel we wanted to play pickleball," her mother told her father.

"Yes, but as long as I have a pro to play with, I'd like to play a tennis game with Mike." Her father smiled at him. "I brought my racket."

"Sure. Let me know when you're available, and I'll work it around my schedule," said Mike.

Hazel and her mother exchanged glances. It was clear that her father was making an effort to get to know Mike.

"Tell me about the posters in the guest room," said Hazel's mother.

Hazel caught her breath and then said, "You know about Jed, the boy that I've grown very fond of? He's in the foster care system and has a safe home with his foster parents. But his life with them may be in jeopardy. Both Mike and I want to take him in if he can't move to Pennsylvania with the rest of the family. Even if he can move with them, there may be a time when we would need to care for him until his move."

"I see," said her mother. "So, the boy would stay in your guest room?"

"Yes, but there's more to it than that," said Hazel. She looked at Mike.

"I grew up in the foster care system in Florida," said Mike. "When I learned that Hazel was interested in fostering a child, Jed in particular, I was deeply touched. I guess you could say that the boy brought us closer. Now, we're thinking that we want to do it together."

Hazel's father frowned. "Are you even engaged?"

Mike looked very uncomfortable.

"We've talked about a future together," said Hazel. "We just haven't had time to put our lives in order."

"In truth, I was waiting to meet you," said Mike to her father. "Isn't that how it usually goes?"

"We need to be able to do things in our own time," said Hazel. "It's a bit upside down, but that's how we want it."

"Are you saying you would foster a child before you were even committed to one another?" asked Hazel's mother with alarm.

"Only Jed," said Hazel. "If we're not needed for him, we'll hold off on taking in other children until we've had a normal engagement, wedding, and time to settle. Mike has bought a home in The Meadows and will take ownership of it soon."

Her parents turned to him.

"What about your work as a tennis pro in Florida?" her

mother asked Mike.

"It doesn't mean I won't travel there from time to time, but I've decided to make Lilac Lake my home," he said.

"And he could travel to other places as well," said Hazel. She knew he was going to play in some smaller tournaments.

"Well then, we guys will make an effort to spend some time together while I'm here," said her dad amiably.

Hazel didn't realize her hands had become sweaty until she almost dropped her wine glass when she lifted it to take a sip.

Her mother gave her an understanding look and held up her glass in a kind of salute. "We women need some time together, too."

After her parents got their things settled in their room, Hazel and Mike prepared dinner.

Mike grilled the steaks, and Hazel made a salad and heated a potato casserole.

"I told your father you were learning to cook," Hazel's mother said to her as they ate. "This is delicious. And I love that Mike did the grilling."

Dad said to Mike, "It's a man's job. Right?"

Mike nodded, but Hazel could see the surprise on his face at being included.

"Elliott wants to have you for dinner. Maybe tomorrow night," said Hazel. Her parents glanced at one another.

"I think it's wise for Elliott to spend time with your father. It certainly helped me," said Helena.

"You know, people might think I had it easy growing up in my family where they determined my future and I had no financial worry," said her father. "But I've had to earn my spot in the company, start at the bottom, and work hard to get where I am."

"You've given us a very comfortable life," said Hazel's mother. "And we appreciate it."

"Well, I appreciate how Mike has worked hard for his professional career," said Hazel, giving him a look of approval.

"Yes, that's very admirable," said her father. "So, you were in the foster care system most of your young life?"

"Yes, sir," said Mike. "It's one reason Hazel and I have such an interest in helping Jed and others in the future."

Hazel's father studied her and then gazed at Mike, before nodding.

Pleased by her parents' open attitudes, she glanced at her mother, who gave her a subtle wink, and Hazel knew she was thrilled with the idea of a future wedding.

CHAPTER TWENTY-FOUR

THE NEXT MORNING, INSTEAD OF GOING TO THE SPORTS Center for practice, Hazel stayed at home with her parents while Mike left to give a tennis lesson.

"I think I'll walk into town," said her father.

"In that case, Hazel and I will have time for our girl talk," said her mother. "Having coffee on the deck at this time of day is lovely."

"Before you go, let me suggest having breakfast at the Lilac Lake Café. Their food is wonderful," Hazel told her father.

"That sounds about perfect," he responded. "I'm usually on the golf course at this hour, but the walk will be an interesting alternative."

"Have fun," said Hazel, seeing him out the door.

She returned to the kitchen, grabbed a cup of coffee, and went out to the deck to join her mother.

"What's going on? It seems as if Dad has been prepped for the visit," Hazel said.

"Your father and I had a very productive talk on our flight," her mother said. "Believe it or not, it's hard to find some time together with each of us so busy. I told him about the conversation Elliott and I had, my meeting with Mike, and the need for us to be accepting."

"I see," said Hazel, unable to hide her surprise.

"Your father wasn't wrong when he said he had his future

planned by his parents. Both of us fell into those plans, and we've had a rewarding life together. But after my visit here, I realized how old-fashioned that whole concept is. You and Elliott were supposed to get married. Why? Because it would've been perfect for the social status of both families. I'm ashamed to admit it."

"I love Elliott, and if he weren't gay, I might have married him," said Hazel. "But I've known since we were kids that it would never happen. And, Mom, with Mike, I've finally learned what love is. I've never felt this way about anyone else. It's as if we click together. You know?"

"Yes, I do," said her mother. "I see how you look at one another, the way he sometimes just touches your hand. It's the sweetest thing ever."

"I thought Dad was going to be difficult about Mike's background," Hazel said.

"As long as he knows Mike will never hurt you and will do his best to care for you, he'll have no objection to you and Mike being together." Her mother's smile lit her eyes. "He's pretty excited about playing a game with a pro like Mike."

"Mike and I have talked about our future together, but he hasn't proposed. Neither one of us wants to feel pressured into anything," said Hazel, giving her mother a warning look.

"I'm glad. Now, tell me about the house Mike has bought. Is it in town?" her mother said.

"It's outside of town some distance away. After we get dressed, I'll take you there, and on the way back to town, we can stop at the Lilac Lake Inn for lunch."

"I'd love that. I've missed our girl times," said her mother.

"Me, too," said Hazel, realizing she had. All her girlfriends in town had helped fill that space, but she was enjoying her mother in a new way.

The drive out to The Meadows allowed her mother to see the lake in its entirety.

"The scenery is beautiful," gushed her mother. "I wonder if it's easy to find a rental in the summertime. That way, your father and I could stay for longer without bothering you kids."

"While we're at the Meadows, I can introduce you to Melanie Perkins, a real estate broker. She can tell you more about rentals. Just be careful to be discreet. She's the holder of every bit of news in town. I think that's why she's so successful. She knows of houses coming on the market before they're ever put there."

Her mother chuckled. "I promise not to mention an engagement between you and Mike."

"Don't say anything about us being together or she'll not only have us engaged, she'll have us married," said Hazel. "Sound like someone you know?"

"Not anymore, remember?" her mother said gently but firmly.

"I'm glad I'm sharing this day with you," Hazel said, glancing her mother's way before returning her eyes to the road.

She drove through the entrance to The Meadows and parked in front of the sales office. "Come with me, and you can talk to Melanie."

As soon as they stepped inside, Melanie stood behind her desk. "Ah, Hazel, is this your mother? I heard she was in town."

Hazel couldn't help grinning. Melanie already had the news. "Yes. This is my mom, Helena Belmont. She'd like to ask you a few questions about rentals in the area and then we're going to drive by Mike's new house. Any word on when the family is moving out?"

"Soon. And I understand the interior will be painted before he moves in," said Melanie. "So, it'll be a few more weeks before he's ready to live there." She offered them seats and after going through her files, she handed Hazel's mother several sheets of paper showing rentals in the area.

"The best thing to do is rent a season ahead," said Melanie. "These will give you an idea of the size and pricing for several rental properties in the area. Several are used as summer rentals and again for winter rentals for the ski season."

"Thank you," said Hazel's mother.

"Have you seen the interior of Mike's house yet?" asked Melanie. "The family is there now, which is why you can't go inside unless you make an appointment."

"No, we're just going to drive by today," said Hazel. "I wanted Mom to see it. That's all."

"Okay, then," said Melanie, picking up her ringing phone. "See you later."

Hazel and her mother got into her car, and she drove up the street into the upscale neighborhood. "There's a community boathouse and club for the residents. It's where a lot of people keep their canoes. Only motorboats with small engines are allowed on the lake to keep the area quiet and not disturb the wildlife."

"A great idea," said her mother.

Hazel stopped in front of the house Mike had bought. Seeing it again, knowing that one day she might live there, Hazel looked at it with fresh eyes. It was a beautiful home.

Seeing the toddler and older child playing in the front yard, Hazel wondered if that's what it would look like when she and Mike owned it.

"It's a lovely house. The entire neighborhood is beautiful. And look, it's delightful to see children playing. An appealing place for growing families."

"The ex-governor and his wife live in the woods at the far end of the development. And there's Melissa and Ross Roberts' house," said Hazel.

Her mother gazed at everything with delight. "I admire your cabin on the river, but this is much better for a family."

"I agree," said Hazel. "But the cabin has served me well. I love being in the center of everything."

"Yes, Lilac Lake is such a charming town."

"Ready for lunch?" Hazel asked. "We'll stop at the Inn. The Inn was owned by Genie Wittner, the Gilford girls' grandmother, GG. She was forced to sell it but retained some acreage and a cottage on the property, which she has given to her granddaughters, who are friends of mine."

"Interesting," said her mother. "Is their grandmother still alive?"

"Oh, yes," Hazel said, smiling. "She's the grand dame of the area, the sweetest, most generous woman ever. She's always doing something kind for someone. On another visit, I'll try to arrange for you two to meet."

"Where does she live?" her mother asked.

"She moved to The Woodlands, an assisted living facility

at the edge of town. You met Brad and Aaron Collister. Their company was the main contractor for its construction."

"I just love how everyone is connected," said her mother.

"It took a while to get used to small-town living, but I like it now," admitted Hazel.

She pulled into the parking lot for the Inn.

Hazel and her mother got out and stood momentarily, inhaling the smell of pine and something undefined but fresh coming from the lake.

They walked up to the front of the building, which still held some of the original fixtures and finishing touches from the original inn.

Inside, an antique reception desk made a bold statement in the contemporary lobby.

A sign pointed them in the direction of the dining room, and they headed there.

On this summer day, the dining room was crowded with hotel and regional guests alike, distinguishable by their attire.

A hostess took the information and led them to a table for two overlooking the front lawn.

Hazel made sure her mother got the best seat for a view out the window.

After a waitress had given them menus and filled their water glasses, she left.

Hazel pointed outside. "Across the lake, you'll see a large gray house. That belongs to the Grahams. Someday, David and my friend, Misty, will live there. His parents want to retire soon."

"How are the winters here?" asked her mother.

"They're cold, for sure," Hazel said. "Summer is a better

time for you to visit."

"I do enjoy warmth," said her mother. "Now, what are you going to order?"

"I'm going to order clam chowder and a salad," said Hazel. "Their clam chowder is fabulous summer or winter."

"Okay, that's what I'll order too," said her mother, setting down her menu on the table and gazing out the window. "Oh, look! A cardinal! How pretty."

"We have lots of birds," said Hazel. "I've been meaning to buy a bird feeder."

"I'll get you one. Where's the best place?"

"At Beckham's Lumber Company. Beth Beckham has a shop there that has everything. Otherwise, Bullard's Hardware Store has them too."

"Okay, let's make a stop at either place on our way home," said her mother.

"Deal," said Hazel. She'd pick something suitable for both the river and Mike's new house.

"I've been meaning to ask how Cassandra is dealing with Elliott's news," said Hazel. "He has a boyfriend and seems to be very happy."

"She's doing a lot better. Both of his parents are. They love him, of course."

"I know. That's why it was so sad that Elliott never felt he could tell them the truth. It will be helpful for you and Dad to have dinner with him tonight," said Hazel.

"Yes, he texted me this morning, and I confirmed it," said her mother. "That will give you and Mike an evening together without us. But tomorrow, I thought it would be fun for your father to go to Jake's. He'll get a real taste of the town. I loved it."

"Okay, that's easy enough to do," said Hazel, pleased by her mother's enthusiasm. This visit was going so well, she hoped nothing would break this spell.

Just as they were getting in her car. Her cell phone rang. *Lisa.*

"Hi, Lisa, what's up?" she asked.

"It's Jed. Any chance you and Mike can have him stay with you next week? It'll be for a week, maybe a day or two more, while my husband and I find a new house in Pennsylvania. Janis, next door, will stay here with the two youngest, but I thought this would be practice for you and Mike, should it come to you fostering him."

"Sure, that won't be a problem. My parents are in town but will leave in a few days, so we should be able to do it."

Hazel ended the call and caught her lip. Her life was about to change in a big way.

CHAPTER TWENTY-FIVE

When Hazel and her mother returned to the cabin, Mike and her father were getting ready to go to the Sports Center to play some tennis.

"How nice," said her mother. "Do you mind if Hazel and I watch?"

"Not at all," her father said confidently. He was talented at both golf and tennis.

Mike shrugged. "Fine with me."

They all loaded into Mike's car and drove to the Center.

"What do you think of Mike and Ross's project?" Hazel asked her father.

"It's quite an operation. Very impressive," he answered.

"We had a lovely trip to see Mike's new house and stopped at the Lilac Lake Inn for a delicious lunch," said Hazel's mother. "I am liking Lilac Lake more and more."

"The town is very attractive," her father said. "I had breakfast at the Café, looked around town, and walked over to the Sports Center to meet Mike for lunch. Everyone was friendly."

As they all got out of the car, a little girl who looked to be about ten years old ran over to Mike. "Hi, Mike. I'm doing better with my serve. Want to see?"

"Sure. Come get me when it's time for your next lesson," said Mike. "Did Paco show you how?"

The girl nodded. "Mallory, too."

"Okay," said Mike, smiling at the girl before she ran off. "Paco and Mallory are our new hires," explained Mike to her parents. "I'm glad to see the kids like them. It's important."

"There was one instructor here who didn't seem very likable," said Hazel's mother.

Hazel didn't dare mention Tracy's name.

"I know who you mean," said Mike. "She's no longer working for us. C'mon, Ray, let's get ready to hit the court."

Hazel and her mother sat on a bench outside the tennis courts to watch the match.

Hazel's mother turned to her. "Your father likes to win."

"Mike is very generous in giving his opponents a fair chance," said Hazel. "When I play tennis with him, he's very sweet about letting me have opportunities to score."

"You were an excellent player in college," said her mother.

"I'm even better now. I've learned a lot from him." Hazel grinned and cast an admiring glance at Mike.

Her mother put an arm around her. "You're sounding more like a woman in love every day."

The men seemed well-matched to begin with, but then Mike took over by placing some shots that were impossible to return. It was interesting for Hazel to see how in control Mike was without being too flashy. She clapped and cheered for both of them, delighted to see how well Mike and her father seemed to be getting along.

After a couple of sets, the men's match on the court was over.

"Time for me to cool off," said her father, taking a sip of water.

"Let's go back and relax at the house for a while before we head to Elliott's for dinner," said Hazel's mother.

"Okay, excellent game, Ray," said Mike. "If you don't mind, I'll drop you off at the cabin and come back here for a private lesson I couldn't rearrange."

'I'll stay here and return home with you after your lesson," Hazel told Mike. "I need to check on a few things so I can have the afternoon off tomorrow."

"No problem. Your father and I appreciate the time both of you are making for us," said her mother.

Alone in her office, Hazel checked her messages, made sure the calendar was up to date for tomorrow's activities, went into the store to check on sales there, and moved outside to make sure the trash cans had been emptied on schedule and went to talk to the lifeguards at the pool to be sure they were on the schedule for the rest of the week. Morning exercise and swimming classes were filling up, and people were already asking about winter classes.

Slowly, but surely, the number of employees was rising. Keeping track of them was becoming a real issue because each one served a different purpose, a different sport at a different time.

She ran into Ross, who was supervising a junior baseball team match-up with some older kids.

"They're looking better," she said, stopping to say hello.

"It's rewarding to see how much they're growing with each game. It's pretty low-key now, but it will be a very different scene in the winter, when we offer serious training for professionals. That's when I'll be super busy."

"The Sports Center is growing very well," said Hazel. "Paco and Mallory seem to be doing a commendable job. That's a huge help. But I'm going to need to hire someone as my assistant soon."

Ross gave her an approving nod. "Yes, Ma'am. Mike and I were talking about that the other day."

"Well, I have to go," said Hazel. "My parents are here."

"How's that going? What do they think of Mike?" he asked.

"So far, it's been okay," said Hazel. "He's doing his thing, just being himself."

"He's solid," said Mike.

"Let's hope it keeps up. Mike just beat my father at tennis."

Mike laughed. "That's one way to make an impression."

At the memory of Mike's victorious grin, Hazel chuckled. Both her father and Mike had a lot of pride, but the match seemed to work to keep things open and friendly between them.

That evening, after seeing her parents off to visit Elliott, Mike wrapped an arm around Hazel and drew her close. "Alone at last."

She leaned against him, smelling the lemony soap he'd used for a shower. "It's important that we have this bit of breathing time away from my parents. We need to talk about a phone call from Lisa. I didn't want to do it in front of my parents."

Hazel filled him in on the details. "So, next week we'll have Jed for probably a week. After talking to her, I have the feeling that Lisa and her husband will be able to keep Jed. With a foster parent shortage in each state, I can't imagine them being denied."

"I think you're right," said Mike. "I just want to make sure it happens. I'm willing to step in and take Jed if it becomes necessary."

"Me, too," said Hazel. "It's something we've always agreed on. By the way, I was impressed seeing your house again through my mother's eyes. It's beautiful and in a nice neighborhood for children."

"No matter what happens, it's a smart investment," said Mike, bursting Hazel's bubble of the images she'd conjured up of the two of them living there with a family.

Hazel told herself to slow down such thinking. A lot could happen in the next couple of weeks as they took on their first foster child, if only for a week.

"Let's skip dinner for now. I have a better idea," Mike murmured in her ear, and all thoughts of any trouble disappeared as Hazel gazed up at him and said, "Me, too."

Later, still energized from their lovemaking, Hazel put together a salad while Mike grilled some chicken breasts out on the deck. Observing him from this vantage point, Hazel could imagine what it might be like someday. It almost scared her that this visit with her parents was going that well and that Mike seemed at ease with them. He'd told her he'd fight for her. Maybe this was how he was doing it. She set places at the kitchen bar for them and went out to the deck to check on the chicken. "Everything's ready inside. How are we doing here?"

"Almost ready," said Mike. "I have been thinking about

tomorrow. I have an early morning meeting with Ross, then I'm going to pick up Jed to see if we can get in some time for him to practice. The doctor has given his go-ahead for Jed to run on that ankle, but we don't want him to twist it. I've found a brace he can use on it."

"My parents have a couple of morning sessions to play pickleball, and then they want to take some time on their own to look around the area. So, I'll be at the office most of the day but will try to get out to watch you and Jed practice."

"Then, we're all going to Jake's. Right?"

"Yes," said Hazel. "I'm anxious for them to spend time with our friends."

Mike loaded the chicken breasts onto a platter and brought it inside.

Hazel poured them each a glass of chilled Pinot Grigio and served up the salad.

As they were eating, their parents returned.

"My! You're eating late," said her mother.

"We had lots to talk over," Hazel said, willing herself not to blush. Her parents didn't need to know that she and Mike had enjoyed a sensational time of making love.

"Help yourself to chicken," said Mike.

Hazel's father laughed. "I'm stuffed. Elliott served us a delightful meal of lake trout."

"Sounds delicious," said Hazel.

"It was, and a good time was had by all," said her mother, smiling with satisfaction. "I'm really glad that we had time with him. Aren't you, Ray?"

Hazel's father nodded agreeably. "It was nice to see him happy."

"That's all any parent wants—for their children to be happy," said Hazel's mother. "That's why this visit has been such a pleasure."

"It's going to be a busy day tomorrow," said Hazel. "Remember, we're going to Jake's for dinner."

"I'm delighted to have the chance to meet more of your friends," said her mother. "I'm going to sit outside for a bit, and then I'm coming to bed."

"If you don't mind, I'm going right to bed after I clean up the kitchen," said Hazel. "Like I said, it's going to be a busy day. Can I get you water, coffee, or wine?"

"Nothing for me, thanks," said her mother.

"I'll have a beer," her father said. "Then, I'm going to sit with your mother. I like this cool, clean air."

"Goodnight," said Mike. "I'll help Hazel with the kitchen, and then I'm going to bed. I have a very early morning meeting with Ross. It's the only time we seem to have for them."

Mike shook hands with her father with confidence, and she felt as if he'd come a long way.

Later, in bed, she told him so. But he shook his head. "I have a distance to go to match the kind of life you've had."

"But I want a life with you, no matter what that might look like," said Hazel, suddenly worried.

"I want you now," said Mike playfully, leaving her with unsettled feelings even as he kissed her.

CHAPTER TWENTY-SEVEN

THE NEXT DAY WAS AS BUSY AS EVERYONE HAD PLANNED. When it came time to go to Jake's, Hazel, her parents, and Mike were ready to sit and relax.

"Mom's already been to Jake's, but Dad, I'm anxious for you to meet everyone. My friends are the so-called 'movers and shakers' of this small town. I think you'll enjoy meeting them."

"It's a lovely group of friends," said her mother.

"I'm looking forward to it," her father said.

Hazel was glad to see most of her friends were already sitting at the locals' tables when they walked into the bar. She waved and led her parents over to them.

After she'd introduced her parents and saw that they were seated, she sat in an empty chair next to Misty. She nudged her. "I showed Mom the house where you and David might live after his parents retire."

"It might be sooner than we thought. David's father is suffering from arthritis in his knees, and he can't wait to get to Florida." She shook her head. "There's always something happening. Who would've thought you and Mike would be together? At one time, you weren't interested."

"I've gotten to know the real him, and I'm definitely interested." She glanced at Mike talking to her Dad and felt a spark of happiness zing through her. Everything seemed to be falling into place.

The group was full of news of the town's activities. As usual, the Labor Day Weekend was a time for picnics and barbeques throughout the town. This year, the high school was putting on a band concert on the town green, and the local summer drama club was presenting a play about the origin of Lilac Lake.

Hazel turned to Whitney. "Were you in charge of the play?"

"For most of the summer, until my sweet baby girl, Lily, arrived."

Hazel and Whitney exchanged smiles.

Hazel's mother seemed happy talking to Taylor about books, and her father was now talking to Gage about veterinarian matters. She felt Mike's eyes on hers and returned his grin. She'd loved having her parents visit, but now she couldn't wait for some alone time with him.

The next morning, Hazel woke to see her parents off to Boston for their return flight home. Mike had already left the house to give a tennis lesson, leaving Hazel to feel like a little girl again with her parents as she went outside with them to say goodbye.

Her father had his turn for a hug, giving her a big squeeze before pulling away and giving her a misty-eyed gaze. "Take care, Hazel. You know I'm always here for you."

"I know. Thanks, Dad," she said, feeling as if she were young again, and headed off to her first overnight camp.

"Say goodbye again to Mike for us. We enjoyed spending time with him," said her mother, hugging her again before sliding onto the passenger seat of their rental car.

"I will," said Hazel. She stood and waved as they pulled out of the driveway.

That night, when Mike was due to come home, Hazel was ready for him, wearing a swishy pink sundress he liked. In the kitchen, a bottle of white wine and a cheese and fruit tray waited for them.

When he walked into the house and saw her, he grinned. "Don't you look delicious?"

She laughed. "I thought we'd enjoy this evening together because Lisa called to say they will leave early. The day after tomorrow, we'll get Jed."

"Guess there's no holding back on that plan of ours," Mike said. "It'll be a real test to see how we handle it."

"Yes, I guess it will," said Hazel. "I'm glad we'll have a few nights alone before he comes to us."

He wrapped his arms around her. "Let's not waste a minute. I'm going to take a quick shower, but I might need some assistance."

"I'm happy to help," said Hazel. She and Mike hadn't done more than kiss and cuddle with her parents at her house, and she was ready for more. A lot more.

Later, after drying off, she dropped her towel and embraced Mike, loving the feel, the clean smell of him.

He rubbed her back and murmured, "I'm glad to have you to myself."

They dressed and went into the kitchen, where they poured wine into two glasses and took the appetizers out on the deck.

"I heard from the realtor today. I can take over the house

in a week. I've already talked to a paint contractor for Collister Construction about painting the interior. He also liked your idea of a softer, warm gray for the walls. With all the light from the windows in the house, he thought it was a better choice than white."

"I'm glad. It will blend the interior much better in that open space," said Hazel.

"Will you help me furnish the house?" asked Mike.

"Of course. But we'd better not wait. Some of it will have to be ordered. Maybe we should drive to Concord. There are a couple of design and furniture stores there that you should probably check out."

"Okay, I'll cancel a couple of classes in the afternoon when it's hot and we can go," said Mike. "I don't want anything to interrupt our time with Jed."

The next afternoon, Hazel and Mike took off for their furniture shopping. Typical of Hazel, she'd made a list of things he'd need. The furniture he had in Florida would be left with the condo to be rented out. The condo here would remain for Paco and Mallory's use.

As they drove, Hazel talked to Mike about her ideas and what kind of look he might prefer.

They both knew what they liked when they pulled into a new furniture store in town.

Hazel had made an appointment with a designer, and she met them when they walked into the store.

"Hi, I'm Eloise, here to help you. You must be Mike and Hazel. I recognized the tennis outfit."

"Sorry," said Mike. "I didn't have time to change. Hazel

and I have been talking, and what we like is what Hazel calls comfortable contemporary."

Eloise, a tall, elegant-looking woman with silver hair pulled back into a bun, smiled. "I'm sure we can find exactly what you need. Hazel said the interior of your house will be done in a pale, but warm gray. Excellent."

Walking through the huge store and going from one room setting to another was initially confusing until Eloise noted how one item might be used with another.

"Keeping the color tones on the neutral side will allow you to use a pop of color here and there for excitement," Eloise said.

After three hours, Mike was ready to stop. "Okay, I trust the two of you to come up with a plan. You both know what I like. And Hazel, you can choose whatever you want." He looked at Eloise. "I'm hoping Hazel will live there with me one day."

While Mike answered his cell, Hazel sat down with Eloise to draw up a list of items.

"I'll email the list to you both," said Eloise. "But, Mike, we need your signature and a deposit."

Hazel got up and walked away while Mike took care of the finances. They'd done a lot of work in selecting furniture, but the process of furnishing the house was far from done.

They drove back to Lilac Lake in silence.

Hazel was almost asleep when Mike said, "I meant what I said, Hazel. I want you to live in my house with me."

"I know," she answered.

"Hey, what's wrong?" asked Mike.

"Are we going too fast? Too early? To be making this kind of decision?" she asked.

"What are you saying? Are you backing out of any plans for us?"

"No, no, but I don't want to get hurt. You know how I feel about you ...

"Yes, and I feel the same about you," said Mike. "So, what's the problem?"

"I don't know. Maybe I'm just tired," said Hazel, feeling confused by all the changes in her life.

He reached over and took hold of her hand. "You know how much I care."

She nodded.

"So, let's go home and relax. Or better yet, how do you feel about pizza?"

"Pizza sounds wonderful. I'll order it online now, and we can pick it up on our way into town," said Hazel, telling herself not to worry about details. Mike loved her and that's all that mattered.

CHAPTER TWENTY-EIGHT

The next morning, Hazel and Mike stood at the door to the guest room, looking in.

"The posters look great," said Mike. "And I like the books you placed on Jed's bed."

She turned to him. "And the tennis balls you put there." She squeezed his hand affectionately. They were both looking forward to having Jed with them and had decided to split their days in the coming week so he would be with one of them at all times. If an emergency arose, they had a babysitter living at The Woodlands who'd help them out.

Hazel checked her watch. "He should be here any moment." She straightened her blouse and drew a deep breath.

At the sound of the doorbell, they both rushed to the door.

Hazel opened it to see Jed holding his tennis racket in one hand and a canvas bag holding his belongings in the other. She'd heard that a lot of foster kids had plastic garbage bags to hold their things, and was happy to see that it was different for Jed.

Lisa got out of the car and walked up to the front door. "Jed was too excited to wait for me. Right, Jed?"

Jed grinned. "It's a big sleepover. Like going to camp."

"Not exactly," said Hazel, tousling his hair. "But we're going to have a fun time."

"We'll call to check on him. We're waiting to hear news

from the system. It's looking positive, a matter of a day or two for the final approval. We'll let you know." Lisa tousled Jed's hair and gave him a quick hug. "Behave for Hazel and Mike. We'll be back soon."

From the car, Lisa's husband, Joe, waved and gave a little beep of the car's horn before pulling out of the driveway.

Jed stood with Mike and Hazel, waving until the car was out of sight.

"Come on in," said Mike. "We'll show you to your room."

"Are you hungry?" asked Hazel. "I've got cookies and milk in the kitchen."

Jed looked at Mike and followed Hazel.

"Guess I can't compete with cookies," softly grumbled Mike.

"We're going to have a pleasant time," said Hazel, watching Jed dig into a cookie and sip milk. "You'll get to go to work with Mike and me sometimes."

"I've bought you tennis balls," said Mike.

"And there are a few new books on the bed for you," said Hazel. "C'mon. We'll show you to your room. You can bring a cookie with you."

Mike led them down the hallway and stopped at the doorway to the guest room. "What do you think? Aren't the posters cool? We got them just for you."

"I'll help you settle your things," said Hazel. "You can put your clothes in the bureau."

Jed stood by while Hazel lifted his things out of the bag. Looking at how worn they were, she had an impulse to go out and buy him a whole lot of new clothes. But she wouldn't do that to Lisa and her husband. They were doing their best to take care of Jed. They loved him.

"I'm going to let you watch me teach tennis to an adult, and then you're going to participate in an intermediate kids' class," said Mike. "Your ankle is doing well."

"Yes, it's all better," said Jed.

"Okay, let's go," said Mike, clapping Jed on the back. "Hazel will catch up with us there."

"Yes, I'll take care of a few things here and then meet you. Because the weather is supposed to become rainy, the tennis camp kids will watch a movie inside. You can join them."

"Cool," said Jed, beaming at her.

Hazel hugged him. "Have fun with Mike."

After Mike and Jed left, Hazel returned to the guest room and added a teddy bear wearing a tennis outfit to the top of the bedspread. There was so much she wanted to do for Jed, but she knew she shouldn't go overboard. She and Mike had already confused Jed by competing for his attention.

She cleaned the kitchen, gathered her things, and left for work.

At the Sports Center, she was soon caught up in answering questions, making phone calls, placating people who hadn't signed up for courses in time, and dealing with the problems of running the Center.

She peeked into one of the gyms to see Jed watching a movie with other kids and was pleased to see him sitting with friends.

She, Mike, and Jed had lunch together in her office picnic style, and then Jed sat in her office playing games on his phone.

"Are you having fun?" she asked him.

He nodded. "I almost won."

She chuckled and went back to a project she was working on, content to see him relaxed with her.

By the time they were ready to return to the cabin, Hazel knew they'd have to do something different for the next day. Maybe Lucille Nordby, Sarah's babysitter from The Woodlands, could take Jed to the movies. She'd check.

Later, when Mike came home, both Hazel and Jed rushed to greet him.

He gave Jed hearty pats on the back, exchanged a fist bump with him, and then turned to Hazel to kiss her. "How's it going, you two?" Mike asked Jed before pulling Hazel into an embrace.

"Good," said Jed, glancing at Hazel in Mike's arms.

"Fine," Hazel said. "I now have a new kitchen helper to set the table."

Jed nodded proudly.

"We're going to have dinner soon," said Hazel. "Jed is used to eating early."

Mike looked at his watch and frowned. "Okay, what's for dinner?"

"Hot dogs. Jed's favorite," said Hazel, tousling Jed's hair.

Mike twisted his mouth but didn't say anything before walking away to shower and change.

Later, after dinner, while Jed was watching television, Mike said to Hazel, "Look, I'm happy to have hot dogs one night, but Jed is our guest, and he needs to eat what we do. Something like chicken or steak—hearty and healthy."

"But he's not used to the fancy food we like," said Hazel.

She indicated the living room with a nod of her head. "Why don't you watch some television with Jed?"

"Okay, it's been a rough day for me, and I can use the downtime," said Mike.

Hazel finished cleaning up in the kitchen and went to join the guys in the living room. A movie with gunmen was on the screen.

She frowned and said, "Hey, no violence. Let's watch something different."

"Sorry," said Mike. "It's not bad. The show is almost over, and we want to see the rest of it. Right, Jed?"

"Yeah, it's a cool show. I've never seen it before," said Jed.

"Of course not," grumbled Hazel.

Mike gave her a questioning look.

Aware there was no option, she sat down with them for a satisfactory ending. While the show was interesting for her as an adult, Hazel thought it was something Jed didn't need to see. She gripped her arms in front of her and stewed.

When the show ended a few minutes later, Hazel said, "Okay, Jed. Time for a bath and then bedtime."

"Lisa doesn't make me take a bath," said Jed.

"Uh, I think you should know that Lisa and I have already discussed the need for you to have a daily bath. So, let's do it," said Hazel in an upbeat tone.

"Awww...okay," said Jed. He ran to his room.

"What's the problem with the show?" Mike asked.

"Violence desensitizes children. Their brains are still developing until they reach their twenties or so. Watching something like that show is considered dangerous to them. Something I learned when I was teaching," said Hazel.

"I'm sorry," said Mike. "It won't happen again."

Jed appeared in the hallway. "Are you coming?"

"I'll get the water going. You grab your pajamas," said Hazel pleasantly, determined to get this visit off to a proper start.

Jed left them again, and Mike turned to her. "Maybe this once, he could've gone without a bath."

Hazel shook her head. "No," she said in a firm tone. "We have to keep to a schedule."

"Don't be a hardass," said Mike with a seriousness she couldn't deny.

Not wanting to get into an argument, she let the comment go. They were both new to this parenting thing and were trying to do an outstanding job.

"Do you want to check on him? Maybe you should see that he has what he needs," said Hazel.

"Sure," said Mike agreeably, and Hazel relaxed a bit.

A short while later, Jed emerged from the bathroom wearing his pajamas. His face shone from a thorough washing.

"Okay, time for bed," said Hazel. "Would you like to read a book before we turn out the light? I'd be glad to read to you."

Jed shook his head "Maybe tomorrow. I'm tired."

"Okay, then," said Hazel, "let's get you settled in bed. Did you see the tennis teddy bear I placed there? That's to make you feel comfortable here."

Jed bit his lip. "Yeah, I like him."

Hazel and Mike walked Jed to the bedroom, and while Mike stood by, Hazel tucked Jed under the light covers.

"We're very happy you're here with us," she said.

"Lisa said she'd call," said Jed, giving her a worried look.

"I'm sure she'll call tomorrow. It's a long drive to Pennsylvania, and they have to have time to get settled. Don't worry. If she said she'll call, she will."

"' Night," Mike said, ruffling Jed's hair.

Hazel leaned over and gave Jed a quick kiss on the cheek.

After they left the room, Mike turned to her. "Ready to relax and watch some more television? I'll let you choose."

"Thanks." She sighed. "I can't believe how tired I am. But I want everything to be comfortable for Jed."

"Aw, Jed's fine," said Mike, and Hazel realized they were very different as parents. Mike seemed a little cold, so matter-of-fact.

When they went to bed, Mike ogled her playfully. "Ready for 'us time'?

"Not tonight. I'm exhausted. But let's cuddle," Hazel said, getting close to him.

Mike drew her closer and sighed.

CHAPTER TWENTY-NINE

HAZEL SAT UP, BLINKING SLEEPILY. SHE CHECKED HER bedside clock. Two A.M.

Getting out of bed, she padded to the guest room and opened the door. The sounds of soft weeping were coming from Jed.

Alarmed, she hurried over to him.

He was curled up on his side, sobbing quietly.

Hazel knelt by the bed and began rubbing Jed's back as she faced him. "Hey, what's the matter?" she crooned.

"At night, Lisa usually sings to me," said Jed. "Is she really coming back? Or will I be left again?"

At the thought of Jed knowing what it was like to be left behind, Hazel's stomach clenched so hard she thought she might be sick. "Oh, Jed, you're not going to be alone again. Lisa and Joe are doing everything they can to make the paperwork complete so you can move with them. She told me it looked positive. She said they're expecting to hear in a day or two."

"Yeah? People have lied to me before," said Jed, sniffling.

Hazel climbed on top of the covers, sat with her head against the headboard, and continued to rub Jed's back.

As she talked softly to him, he nestled against her.

Though she wasn't a good singer, she began humming an old camp song about the moon. Soon, his breathing slowed, and when she looked down, Jed's eyes were closed in sleep.

Studying him, she felt a new, stronger feeling rise in her, the stirring of maternal protection. The thought of anyone hurting a helpless child made her catch her breath. Her eyes grew teary. She didn't know all the particulars of being a parent, but she knew enough to know she'd work hard to keep anything from harming a child in her care.

In the quiet that followed, Hazel climbed off the bed and headed back to her bedroom.

Mike was asleep on his side.

She lay next to Mike, thinking of his childhood and the hurts he must have suffered, and felt her eyes fill with tears again.

Feeling a tenderness, she slid closer to him and felt a sigh escape him when he wrapped an arm across her body.

While he continued sleeping, she lay awake, grateful she'd experienced a stable, loving childhood. The idea of fostering a child remained firmly fixed inside her. She now knew that it wouldn't be Jed, but one day, there would be another who needed her help.

The next morning, Hazel dragged herself out of bed to start the day. Mike and Jed were already in the kitchen.

She padded to them and grinned when she saw that Mike had made coffee, and he and Jed were working together to make eggs and bacon for breakfast. Mike had canceled early morning lessons for the few days Jed would be with them, and it was a relief to see that the day was off to a promising start.

"' Morning, boys!" Hazel walked over to Mike for a kiss and then hugged Jed. "It's going to be an exciting day. Jed, you're going to the movies with me and a very special grandmother. Someone who babysits for a friend of mine. How's that for a surprise?"

"I like movie surprises," said Jed. "Why is she coming with us?"

"Because I want you to get to know her. Later in the week, she's going to stay with you while I attend an afternoon meeting."

Jed frowned.

"If you're not comfortable with her, let me know, and we'll find someone else," Hazel said.

"Okay," said Jed, giving her a solemn look.

"Wish I could go to the movies, too. But now that we have a beautiful day, I'll be out on the courts teaching," Mike said.

"Am I coming to tennis with you?" asked Jed.

"Yes. You can be my ball boy," Mike said.

Jed grinned and gave him a thumbs-up sign.

After Mike and Jed left, Hazel straightened up the house and set the table for dinner. It was going to be a busy day, and she wanted the evening to go more smoothly than yesterday. She was still shaken by Jed's crying during the night and knew a consistent routine might help him.

She went into work with a lighter heart and got busy with some projects for the Fall. She'd learned through teaching how important preparation was. If only she could tell Jed that he'd be allowed to move with Lisa.

Mike took care of lunch with Jed while Hazel finished typing up a report for the board overseeing the Center.

Hazel grabbed a cup of coffee and a cracker to eat as she went to pick up Jed.

Jed was waiting for her outside the Café with Mike as she pulled to the curb.

Mike opened the door for Jed and said, "You two have fun. See you later."

After making sure Jed had his seatbelt on in the backseat, Hazel took off for The Woodlands.

"Ms. Lucy Nordby is the name of the woman we're picking up," said Hazel. "She's excited to meet you. As I told you before, she babysits for a friend of mine and loves children. I think she's lonely, which is why we need to make her feel welcome."

Jed listened intently without speaking.

Hazel pulled up to the front circle of The Woodlands.

A short, blond woman with a curvy and well-kept body got out of a rocking chair on the porch and, smiling, waved at them, then hurried over to the car.

Lucy opened the passenger door and turned to look at Jed in the back seat. "Who is this handsome young man? My date for the afternoon?"

"Lucy, this is Jed. Jed, this is Ms. Lucy," said Hazel.

"I'm always excited to meet new people," said Lucy, sliding onto the passenger seat. "And I love going to the movies. What movie have you picked for us to see, Jed?"

Jed grinned. "It's a new Disney movie."

"Oh, I love that. Thank you for making such an exciting choice," said Lucy. "I have a feeling we're going to get along just fine."

Hazel saw through the rear-view mirror that Jed was nodding his head up and down. She let out a sigh of relief. She didn't mind having the responsibility of caring for Jed, but she liked having a backup person to support her.

Inside the theater, Hazel bought popcorn and water for everyone, and they got seats in the theater showing their film.

As the movie continued, Hazel checked on Jed and was pleased to see a look of delight on his face. She'd gladly work extra hours next week to make up for this time with him.

They'd just dropped off Lucy at The Woodlands when Hazel's cell phone rang. *Lisa.*

"Fantastic news! We just got the okay to transfer Jed to the foster care system in Pennsylvania."

"Oh my God! That's wonderful. Let me put you on the speaker. Jed is in the car with me now."

As Lisa shared the good news all over again, Hazel watched Jed's face light up in the rearview mirror. At the sight of his wide smile, Hazel's eyes filled. She was thrilled for him and for Lisa and her family. Still, she knew she'd miss Jed and wondered how this would affect the relationship between her and Mike. The idea of fostering children is what brought them together.

At home, Hazel went about fixing their dinner. When Mike came in from work, dinner would soon be ready. She'd compromised by making their meal a bit later, knowing Jed had enjoyed popcorn at the movies.

When Mike came into the house, Jed ran over to greet him.

"How's my ball boy? What did you do today?" Mike asked Jed, who stayed by his side as Mike walked into the kitchen to give Hazel a kiss.

"Hi," he said, before pulling away. "I'm going to eat and run right after dinner. I have two couples' matches going on this evening. Hope you don't mind."

"Not at all. Lisa called to say it's all worked out for Jed to move to Pennsylvania. It's going to be a low-key evening for Jed and me to celebrate. We might even read a book together." She glanced at Jed, and he nodded.

A while later, they were sitting at the kitchen table having dinner when Jed said, "I don't feel good."

"You don't have to eat anything more," said Hazel. "You've done quite well. You can go ahead and get started on your bath."

After Jed left the kitchen, Mike said, "He shouldn't waste food."

"I know, but you shouldn't force a child to eat. This has been an emotional time. Thank God, he knows he'll be moving with his family."

"Help!" came a cry from Jed.

Both Mike and Hazel jumped to their feet to see what was going on.

Jed had thrown up all over himself and the bathroom floor and was now kneeling by the toilet.

"Oh, sweetheart, I'm sorry. Let me help you get cleaned up." Hazel pressed a hand to Jed's forehead and rubbed his back. "Did you get it all up?"

Jed gave her a sad nod.

"Well, don't worry about anything. Let's get you in the tub. Take off your outer clothes and then we'll start the water for your bath. In the meantime, I'll start to clean up."

"Hey, Bud, I have to leave for tennis classes, but Hazel will take care of you," said Mike, giving him a pat on the back.

"Stay with him for a moment," said Hazel. "I have to get some cleaning supplies."

She returned to the bathroom with the items she needed, trying not to gag at the smell.

"See you later," said Mike, and gave her a quick kiss.

Left alone with Jed and the mess, Hazel drew a deep breath. This childcare business was harder than she'd thought.

Hazel sat on the edge of the bed, reading to Jed. She'd always loved reading aloud to her students in class and was pleased to see that she'd helped draw Jed into a book about a boy who took a magical trip to the moon.

Jed's eyes began to droop.

Hazel came to a point in the book where she could stop and halt the reading. "We can finish the story tomorrow. Now, you need to get some sleep. Just call out if you need me. I'll keep your door open and mine too. I'll be reading in bed."

"Okay, thanks," said Jed.

"See you in the morning," Hazel said, giving him a quick hug. She'd talked to Jed and realized between what he'd had for lunch, the popcorn, and dinner, that it was not the flu that had made him sick.

When Hazel felt Mike's arms around her, she realized she'd fallen asleep in bed reading. She lifted her head, said hello, and lay down again.

"Hey, I'm going to take a shower. Come join me," he murmured into her ear.

"Not tonight," Hazel said, clinging to her pillow. Romance was definitely out of the question. She was still trying to recover from the effort to remain cheerful and unaffected by the throw-up she'd had to deal with.

CHAPTER THIRTY

THE NEXT AFTERNOON, WHILE SHE WAS MEETING WITH Tom and Evie Jeffries, who owned the sporting goods store in Concord and with whom she'd partnered for clothing at the Sports Center, she hoped Jed was doing fine with Lucy. When she arrived to stay with Jed at the house, Lucy had brought a box full of puzzles, games, and other things to keep them occupied.

After the business portion of the meeting ended, Evie took Hazel aside. "I understand you and Mike Dawson are together. I'm very happy for you. He's a great guy, and I think you'll make a good team going forward."

"I hope so," said Hazel. Recalling the past couple of days, she realized that most of the work of raising kids would go to the mother.

On the way home, Hazel got a phone call from Lisa, telling her they'd be back tomorrow. "How's it going with Jed?"

"It's going well," said Hazel. "But he's attached to you, Lisa. You've done so much for him."

"He's very much a part of our family. I didn't want to have to leave him behind. But now that I know the issue is settled, I'm anxious to move. Joe and I are going ahead and adopting baby Simon and Harry. If we ever get the chance, we'll adopt Jed too."

"What's holding up your adopting him?" Hazel asked.

"Getting the parental releases," said Lisa. "We'll start a fresh search for them in Pennsylvania."

Hazel heard the excitement in Lisa's voice and felt a sting of disappointment. She'd envisioned her future with Mike and Jed. But now she knew she'd have to wait for her future to unfold in its own way.

That night, Mike and Hazel told Jed he could have anything he wanted for his last meal with them. He grinned. "Chicken wings. They're Joe's favorites. Mine, too."

"Then that's what we'll have," said Hazel. "The Chicken Licken restaurant has the best. We'll order those, a salad, and what do you want for dessert?"

Jed's face lit up. "I want their Apple pockets."

"Okay, I'll go get it," said Mike. "Want to ride with me, Jed?"

Jed beamed at Mike. "Yes."

After they left, Hazel searched through her teacher's items and found some paper hats to wear. She wanted Jed to remember his stay here.

The guys returned, carrying packages that emanated wonderful aromas.

"What's this?" asked Mike, picking up one of the hats and putting it on his head.

"Me, too," Jed said, putting on a hat of his own.

Hazel placed one on her head and said, "Okay, let's serve up."

The three of them sat around the kitchen table chatting about a tennis game Jed had played, giving Hazel a glimpse of what having a family might be like.

They finished their meal, and the three of them sat out on the deck. The day's heat had gone, and the birds in the trees were calling out to one another.

"What will you remember most about your stay with us?" Hazel asked Jed.

"Throwing up," said Jed. "I didn't like that."

"Oh, no. I hope you had some happy times here," said Hazel, mortified that's how he'd think of his time with them.

"Oh, yes. I played tennis and went to the movies and read a book with you," said Jed. "Those parts were fun."

"I'm glad," said Hazel, grinning at him.

"You know, if it's all right with Lisa and Joe, you might be able to come to tennis camp and stay with us next summer," said Mike. "We've talked to them about it."

"Really?" said Jed. "I want to be number one at tennis someday."

"It'll take lots of practice to get there, but I believe you have the talent to do it," said Mike. "I'll help in any way I can."

Jed and Mike exchanged long looks, and Hazel was proud of Mike for his commitment to the boy who worshipped him. She knew Mike would follow through.

When it was time to tuck Jed in for the night, both Mike and Hazel made sure he was comfortable. He'd had a bath, had read a book with Hazel, had a last drink of water, and lay in bed staring up at them.

"'Night, sport," said Mike. "See you in the morning. For your last day here, you can join the kids in tennis camp."

"Really?" said Jed.

"We want you to have fun. Lisa will return before

suppertime." Hazel leaned over and gave him a quick kiss on the cheek. "You'll have lots to tell her. Have a good night's sleep."

Hazel and Mike left the room, keeping the door ajar, and slipped out to the deck for some quiet time alone.

"The day after tomorrow, I'm heading south to Florida to take care of some problems and ship some of my things up here. The interior of my house should be painted by the time I'm home, and then the delivery of furniture will begin. I want my first night in the house to be with you."

"I'd love that. It's such an exciting time for you."

Mike grinned. "Growing up, I never dreamed I'd own a house like it."

"It's beautiful," said Hazel. "You should be very proud."

They smiled at one another.

"Let me tell you about my phone call with Lisa. It seems Jed's future is pretty settled. He'll not only live with Lisa and her family in Pennsylvania, but they hope to adopt him. They've already received permission to adopt the two smaller boys. It seems like such a perfect ending for them all."

"I'm happy for them. It often doesn't work out that way."

Hazel heard the sadness in his voice, and her heart went out to him. He was being more open about his past, which she thought was healthy.

"It's going to be another busy day tomorrow," said Mike. "Are you ready for bed?"

His sexy grin sent a surge of anticipation through her. She'd been too tired to even think of making love for the past couple of nights. But maybe tonight...

"Go ahead. I'm going to wash Jed's clothes, so they're all

set for Lisa tomorrow, and then I'll be in."

She tiptoed into Jed's room and gazed at him sprawled across the bed before gathering his clothes. Then, after the washing machine was running, she hurried into her bedroom, anxious for some "Mike and me" time.

She stopped short.

Mike softly snored as he lay atop the covers in his pajama bottoms. Too tired, apparently, even to get under the covers.

So much for any sexy playtime tonight.

The next morning, as Jed's clothes dried, Hazel made sure she put together a fun breakfast of pancakes with raisin eyes and strawberry grins.

Jed's delight made getting up extra early worth it.

Because Mike had already gone to work for an early morning tennis lesson, just the two of them sat in the kitchen talking. "Now that we know you're moving to Pennsylvania, I thought you might like to see it on a map," said Hazel. She lifted her cell phone and showed him a photo of the United States and pointed out where they were now and where Jed would be going.

"As you can see, you only have to go through Massachusetts, Rhode Island, Connecticut, and New York to reach Pennsylvania. So, we won't be that far away."

"Then I can come in the summer."

"If everything is fine with your parents," said Hazel. "But don't worry. I think it'll all work out. We all want the best for you."

"I know," said Jed, and he caught his lip with a flush of emotion.

Hazel hugged him. "You can watch a little television while I get your things ready for camp."

Later, with Jed in camp and Hazel able to work in her office, she thought of an idea for a Christmas event at the Center—a campaign to raise money for scholarships to the children's camps. Jed wasn't the only boy in town who could benefit from that.

While Jed was occupied at the Sports Center with other kids, Hazel left to go home to pack up Jed's things. When it came time for Lisa to pick him up, Hazel wanted it to be a quick transition.

She was delighted that Jed was going back to Lisa's family, and they'd work hard to adopt him. It was a loving home. But it was hard to give up the idea of having Jed permanently after preparing herself for it. Though she'd worked with children while teaching, she'd never attached herself to any child as much as she had with Jed.

Mike and Jed came into the house laughing about something. It was wonderful to see them like this. She knew Mike would miss Jed as much as she did.

They were sitting in the kitchen having a snack when Hazel heard the sound of a car outside. She went to the living room window and looked out. It was Lisa and Joe.

She opened the front door and waited for Lisa to leave the car. Then she went to greet her. "Jed is going to be glad to see you. He's had a good time, but he missed you."

"I can't tell you how relieved I am that we finally have permission to take him with us. We've bought a house big enough for everyone and will move as soon as we sell our house here."

Hazel gazed into Lisa's smiling face, and her eyes misted. "I'm in awe of what you do as a parent. I can't tell you how much I admire you."

"Oh, thank you. That's sweet of you. Don't worry. You'll make a fantastic mother someday."

Arm in arm, they walked into the house. "Jed?" called Lisa.

Jed came running toward them. "You're here!"

Hazel stepped aside while Lisa and Jed hugged.

"You didn't leave me," said Jed, smiling up at Lisa.

Lisa tilted Jed's chin up so he could look directly at her. "No one is going to leave you again," she murmured. "You're very lucky that Hazel and Mike love you, and you can visit them. But your home is with Joe and me and the boys."

Lisa hugged him, and Jed spent a long time hugging her back.

Mike and Hazel exchanged emotional glances.

"I have Jed's things ready to go," said Hazel. "Let me help you carry them to the car."

She and Mike followed Jed and Lisa to the car. After talking to Joe, Hazel handed Jed's things inside to him and then stood by the car with Mike.

"See you at the Sports Center later this week," said Mike.

"Okay," said Jed.

"Have fun at home," Hazel said, faking a bright smile.

As the car pulled out of the driveway, Mike wrapped an arm around her.

Hazel sighed. "The house is going to seem very empty without him."

"I know, but this will give us time before following through with fostering another child. I've realized I'm not ready. Not until things are settled between us."

"I wish you didn't have to go to Florida tomorrow," said Hazel.

"Yes, but now that I can get into my house here, I'm anxious to get my things," said Mike. "And tonight? I want to show a certain someone how much I love her."

Hazel leaned against him, and they walked inside the house together and right into the bedroom.

Later, as they sipped glasses of wine on the deck, Hazel said, "It was heartwarming having Jed here, but I understand why people say to wait to have children until after you've had plenty of time together. Still, I don't want to give up on my dream of having many children with you. And a dog or two. I miss my dachshund at home. It won't seem like a family without one."

The corners of Mike's lips curved. "I love that about you."

Their future held so many possibilities.

The next day, she hugged and kissed Mike and then headed to work feeling very alone. She remembered how her mother had cried when she went off to college and understood better what she must have been feeling.

Being back amid activity helped lift her spirits. And when Dani called her cell to say the gang was meeting at Jake's that evening, she agreed to join them.

Later, as she sat with her friends at the locals' tables, she knew why she loved Lilac Lake as much as she did. They were a friendly, caring, smart group of people.

Everyone asked after Mike, and she told them he was shipping his things from Florida to his new house and that the furniture they'd ordered would be delivered soon.

"I'm delighted to have you as a neighbor," said Melissa. "Ross and I love having Dani and Brad there. It's like one big family."

The conversation turned to the upcoming tennis tournament planned at the Sports Center. Hazel knew that they'd be busy for the foreseeable future between getting Mike's house settled and the tournament.

After she left Jake's and went home, she received a phone call from Mike.

"How are you doing?" he asked. "Still missing me and Jed?"

"Oh, yes. I'm at loose ends. The house is empty and quiet."

"I have a favor to ask. I'm having something delivered to you tomorrow morning at nine o'clock. Can you arrange to be there at the cabin?"

"Sure, but why would you need me to be here?"

"You'll see," said Mike. "I've got to go. I'll talk to you tomorrow."

The next morning, Hazel checked her watch. It was five minutes past nine o'clock, and she worried that her workday would be behind if she was forced to wait for too long for Mike's delivery.

Gage Martens' truck pulled into the driveway.

Puzzled, she went to greet the veterinarian as he climbed

out of his truck. "Morning. What are you doing here?"

He grinned. "I have something for you."

"For me?"

"Yup. Mike called me, and we found the perfect foster dog for you. Come see."

He opened the back door of his truck.

Hazel peered inside and clasped her hands together in delight. "Oh, she's darling."

"She's a six-month-old dapple dachshund who needs a home. Unfortunately, her family couldn't take care of her, and did very little training. But she's bright and eager to please and, like any dachshund, is full of affection. Mike thought you'd be good for her."

Hazel covered her face and let her tears come. She couldn't think of anything sweeter or a better way for Mike to show his love.

"Wha ... what's her name?" Hazel finally asked shakily.

"Her name is Dottie. She's a beautiful dog. All she needs is a loving home."

Hazel reached for the pup and laughed when the dog covered her cheeks with kisses.

Her tail was wagging so fast that Hazel almost dropped her, but then the dog snuggled up against her, winning Hazel's heart forever.

Hugging her tightly, Hazel said, "She's adorable. But I'll need to buy her a blanket and a bed and food and everything."

"I've made a list of what you need," said Gage. "I've checked her over and made sure she has all her shots. So, you should be set to go. The pet store outside of town will have everything you want. And you can call me with any questions you might have."

"What about a leash?" she asked.

"I've got a standard one here for you to match her collar. But you'll want to buy her a harness and a leash with a retractable line. Also, I've put a pamphlet in the bag for you to read."

"Thank you, thank you," said Hazel, her eyes glistening. It seems she was to foster and adopt after all.

CHAPTER THIRTY-ONE

Left alone with the dog, Hazel placed Dottie on the grass and watched as she playfully ran around sniffing the ground. She called the Center and told them she'd be late coming in. Before she could call Mike, he called her.

"Did you get the delivery?" Mike asked.

"Oh, yes! Thank you! She's the best gift ever. I'll send you some pictures of her. Right now, she's sniffing the grass on the front lawn. I'm about to take her out back to the fenced-in area. She's tiny and very smart."

"Are you keeping the name Dottie?" Mike asked.

"It's perfect with her coat of fur. And that face … so cute! I will take her to the pet store with me, and then she can sleep in my office. Gage said she needs training. So, I'll get some puppy pads for emergencies."

"It sounds like you have things under control. Dottie will love being at my house with a big yard to play in."

"I'm warning you that she's going to be a very spoiled puppy. Right now, she is staring at me and …"

"Woof!"

"… barking at me to do something. I'm not sure what, but I'll figure it out. Thank you so-o-o much. I can't think of a more meaningful gift. The timing is perfect, and I love the idea of adopting a pet."

"I know you pretty well and thought this might help you get past the disappointment of not fostering Jed," said Mike, his voice tender.

"Thanks again. Oops! I'd better go. Dottie is running toward the road." Hazel ended the call and sprinted after the dog. Dottie might have short legs, but she could move fast.

Later, loading up her car with store items, it felt like Christmas for a certain pup. She'd bought everything Gage suggested on the list. She hooked up the dog's car seat and strapped Dottie in it so she could see out the window. The back was loaded with not one but two beds, bowls, toys, a harness and a leash, a small crate, and a teddy bear that had a mechanical heartbeat for nighttime comfort.

Hazel got behind the driver's wheel and turned to Dottie. "Here we go! We're off to the first of many adventures."

The dog wagged her tail and barked as if to say okay.

Hazel drove home, dropped off most of the things she'd bought, and then took Dottie and one of her new comfy beds to the office. At six months of age, she was still a baby and would, Hazel hoped, curl up in her bed and go to sleep while she worked.

At the Center, everyone wanted to hold the dog or pet her until Hazel quietly put Dottie in her bed under her desk. The puppy, who was active earlier, slept soundly while Hazel caught up with her work.

The minute Dottie woke up, Hazel hurried her outside. And as the pamphlet suggested, Hazel clapped and fussed over her when Dottie performed.

Prancing with self-adoration, Dottie trotted inside and waited while Hazel got ready to go home. On the way out of the building, Hazel checked with Mallory to make sure the tennis camp was coming to a close for this session and that the new session would start on time.

Seeing Dottie, Mallory got down on her knees to pet her.

Dottie loved the attention, but when Hazel turned to leave, Dottie quickly followed.

At home, Hazel organized everything for the dog, placing a water bowl next to the crate and putting toys and the teddy bear in the crate. Dinner was one of three meals the pup would have, each one a healthy serving of food chosen by Gage.

The one note of warning Gage had given Hazel was to resist letting Dottie out of the crate at night, as she needed to be trained to sleep there. Later, when she was older, they could choose whether to let her in bed, but for now, it was an important part of training.

Hazel read this and looked down at the dog wagging her tail and looking up at her with a doggie grin. Could she do what Dr. Martens asked?

When Mike called to see how she was doing, he asked Hazel, "Are you following Gage's instructions? He reminded me how important it was for Dottie to sleep in the crate at night. I know what a softie you are, but don't give in. Okay?"

"Okay," said Hazel. "She sure is cute. How is your work going there?"

"Fine," said Mike. "I'm packing up my things here, checking on my remaining schedule here in Florida, have some other business to attend to, and will be home in three days."

"We'll both be waiting for you. Me and our baby."

"What?" said Mike, sounding alarmed. "Baby?"

"Our fur baby," Hazel said, chuckling.

They ended the call laughing together.

Hazel sat for a moment, thinking about babies, and turned to the dog. "C'mon, Dottie. We've got to go on an errand."

Back at her house, Hazel sat in her bathroom and stared in dismay at the two lines of the test.

She tried another one.

Two lines appeared again. No doubt about it, she was pregnant.

She knew she couldn't call her mother, and she didn't want any of her friends to know before telling Mike. So, sitting on the floor of the bathroom, Hazel told Dottie all about how she wasn't ready for such news, that it might ruin everything.

Sensing her unhappiness, Dottie climbed into Hazel's lap and licked a tear from her cheek.

Hazel rubbed Dottie's back, recalling the night it might have happened. Mike was usually careful about protection, and she was usually alert about confirming it. But one time, after having too much wine, they must have forgotten. Their lovemaking was that fantastic, Hazel thought, wanting to cry again.

That night, Hazel went to bed alone. Dottie was in her crate in a corner of the room so she could at least see Hazel. Not that it helped to keep the dog from crying.

At the sound, Hazel stiffened and placed a pillow over her head, trying to block out the noise.

Finally, Hazel put in earbuds to listen to some music. Gage had warned her that dachshunds were very stubborn and for her to just tough it out this first night.

The puppy's crying went on and on, rising and ebbing in heartbreaking wails.

Just as Hazel was ready to give up, the room went quiet.

Hazel rose on her elbows to take a look. All she saw was a bundle of the puppy blankets she'd bought lying in the middle of the crate.

Carefully, trying not to make any noise, she climbed out of bed and tiptoed over to the crate. A Dachshund's head lay still inside a twisted bunch of blankets. Eyes closed, Dottie slept.

Sighing with relief, Hazel made her way back to her empty bed. Too tired to stay awake, she turned to her side and clung to Mike's pillow, wishing he was there.

It was early when Dottie stirred and began to cry.

Hazel went to the crate, opened it, and lifted Dottie's warm body into her arms.

"Time for you to go outside, sweetie," crooned Hazel, laughing when Dottie kissed her on the cheek.

Hazel carried the dog to the outside deck and down to the grass.

Dottie did her duty and then sniffed around the fenced yard.

Hazel ran inside to get a robe and slippers and then sat on the deck watching the dog and listening to the songs of birds starting their day.

She still couldn't believe the results of the pregnancy

tests. She felt well, though her breasts were a bit tender.

Her cell phone rang. *Mike.*

"Hi," she said, eager to keep talking about anything but the news of a baby. "Dottie and I had a good night after she cried for almost two hours before falling asleep. This morning, she's having fun in the backyard before we have to get ready to go to work."

"That sounds very promising. The photos of her were spectacular. She sure is cute."

"As Gage said, Dottie wants to please. Maybe training might not be as difficult as I first thought. She knows her name and will come when she's called. But I can see it's going to take work to get her into our routine."

"I thought summer was a wise time to get a dog, so she can play outside," said Mike. "And I knew you'd love having her."

"I really do. She's such a sweet gift. It'll be easier when you're at home to help take care of her. And perhaps you can teach her some tricks," said Hazel, keeping the focus on the dog.

"What are you up to today?" asked Mike.

"One session of tennis camp is ending, and another is beginning. So, I'll be meeting with staff and trying to come up with any new or better ideas about running this next session."

"Hard to believe the summer will soon be coming to an end. Aren't you glad you don't have to prepare to return to school?"

"Yes, I'm very excited about it. Teaching at that school wasn't a good fit for me. Not like the Sports Center," said Hazel. She was now grateful that Principal Nolan Deere had gone psycho on her, nitpicking everything she did, making her want to leave her position at school. It had opened up her life in many ways.

"I've got a few more things to take care of," said Mike. "I'll get them done as quickly as possible and then come home."

"I miss you so much," Hazel said.

"Yeah, I miss you, too," said Mike.

They ended the call.

Hazel sat in the kitchen staring at the wall. Somehow, she had to get through the day while hiding her secret.

CHAPTER THIRTY-TWO

HAZEL TRIED TO CONCENTRATE ON WORK FOR THE NEXT couple of days, waiting for Mike to come home. But her mind kept coming back to those two significant red lines. Neither she nor Mike had explicitly talked about marriage, other than knowing they wanted to be together in the future and wanted to foster a child or have children together one day. She realized now how out of order their plans were. They weren't even engaged. And now she was about to have Mike's baby. Something neither of them had planned nor even talked about wanting right away.

"Everything okay?" Mallory asked her. "You seem distracted, which is not like you at all."

"I'm fine," said Hazel, suddenly feeling sick. "Thanks for asking."

Mike's arrival home couldn't come soon enough. She didn't like hiding secrets from him. Especially this one.

Just before she left the office on the second day, her mother called. "Hi, sweetie! I'm just checking up on you. Your father and I loved the photos of Dottie. What a darling dog. I suppose she'll be a substitute for any grandchildren until you and Mike decide to move forward."

"I suppose so," said Hazel calmly, unwilling to give anything away.

"Your father and I talked about Mike earlier today, and

we both like him a lot," said her mother, nudging Hazel uncomfortably.

"Yes, I like him a lot, too," said Hazel. "I've got to go. Dottie is here at the office with me, and it's time to put her out."

"Oh, of course. We'll talk later," said her mother.

Frowning, Hazel ended the call and stared down at the puppy asleep in her bed.

Thinking of her predicament, her nerves burst into flames inside her body. She'd never felt such uncertainty in her life. How could she face the future when she didn't know how the people closest to her would react to her news?

At home, Hazel had just put Dottie outside and was preparing her dinner when Mike walked into the kitchen.

"You're home," she said, running into his open arms. "I've missed you."

"Me too," said Mike, kissing her.

It felt so thrilling to taste his lips, feel his arms around her. She closed her eyes. The tension she'd felt for the past several days left her, and then suddenly ramped up again.

"Woof!"

Mike dropped his arms and turned as Dottie trotted into the kitchen.

"Hi, pup!" he said, squatting to greet her.

Dottie wagged her tail and leaped into his lap, wiggling to get into position to kiss him.

Laughing, Mike stood holding her. Hanging the pup out in front of him, he grinned. "You're a real cutie. Have you been a good girl for Hazel?"

He turned to her.

"She's been very good," said Hazel. "Gage was right. She's smart and wants to do the right thing for the attention she gets when she obeys."

"Let's drive out to my house. I want to see it, and we can show it to Dottie. I can't wait until it's the three of us living there."

Hazel bit her lip. She wasn't ready to tell him. "Okay, we'll go to your house. I'll bring the dog's food with us."

On the drive, Mike talked enthusiastically about getting his teaching job in Florida scheduled in such a way that it would allow both of them to have winter breaks in warmer weather. I hope you'll be amenable to accompanying me occasionally."

Hazel swallowed hard. She could do that for a while. But after the baby came, it would be harder.

Mike pulled into the driveway of his house, and after getting out of the car, he spent a few moments staring at it.

"It's beautiful," said Hazel, coming up beside him, holding Dottie.

"Come inside. Let's see what they've done," said Mike, moving ahead to unlock the front door.

She stepped inside and gazed around at the pale-gray painted walls and cream trim. "Oh, this is much better. It makes a perfect blend of the rooms."

Dottie wiggled in Hazel's arms. "No, you don't. I'm putting you right outside,"

Hazel walked through the kitchen and out to the screened-in porch, then onto the grass.

When she turned, Mike was beside her, smiling. "Come

inside. The dog will be safe here in the fenced yard. We need to talk."

"Yes, I need to tell you something," said Hazel, allowing Mike to lead her inside, where a couple of bar stools had been placed in front of the kitchen bar.

"Have a seat," said Mike, helping her onto the stool before facing her.

Smiling, he gazed at her. "Hazel, I love you," said Mike. "I've loved you way before we got together this summer. You're the kindest, nicest woman I've ever known. I want you with me now and in all the days to come. Will you marry me?" He pulled a small velvet box out of his pocket to show her a beautiful round diamond ring.

Overcome, Hazel covered her face and sobbed.

"Whoa! The thought isn't that bad, is it?" asked Mike, lifting her chin and giving her a worried look.

"No, it's a wonderful thought, but it won't be just the two of us," said Hazel.

"Of course not. You, me, and Dottie," Mike said.

"Okay, then it'll be the four of us," said Hazel. "I ... I'm pregnant."

The look of shock on Mike's face froze Hazel from her fingers to her toes. It was her nightmare come to life. "You're having a baby?"

She shook her head. "No, *we're* having a baby."

It took her a moment to realize Mike had wrapped his arms around her and was twirling her in a circle, laughing with glee. "Oh, my God! A baby!"

He set her down and cupped her face in his broad hands. "I couldn't love you more."

"I know we hadn't planned on it… " she began.

"It's the ultimate expression of our love," said Mike. "We'll have other children, but this baby will be the beginning of our life together. So, will you marry me?"

Hazel laughed when she realized she hadn't answered him. "Yes, Mike, I'll marry you. *We'll* marry you. You've made me very happy with your response. I was worried that everything was happening too soon."

"It's never too soon for me to have a real home. One with you."

Lifting her hand, she gently wiped a drop of moisture from his cheek. She loved this man and would always give him the home he'd never had as a child.

"I have something to confess," said Mike. "Part of my trip was to meet with your father when he came to Miami on a business trip. I wanted to ask him for your hand in marriage. Just like a real family."

Hazel grinned. "That's why my mother told me they were talking about how much they liked you. Any more surprises?"

"Nope. I think we've covered it all. A ring, a puppy, a house, a baby. Sounds like a perfect plan to me. When's the wedding?"

Laughing, they held onto each other with the promise of a wonderful future together.

EPILOGUE

A few months later, Hazel stood in the master bedroom of the house at The Meadows and gazed at herself in the wall mirror. It was hard to believe that so much had happened to her in such a short time.

She cradled the small bump in her stomach thinking of the baby she was carrying. This little boy, unlike the man she was about to marry, would experience a kind, loving home where he would always know he was loved.

Hazel gazed down at the puppy at her feet. Dottie had been a gift of love and would, she hoped, become a companion for her child.

At the sound of a knock on the door, she called softly, "Come in."

Her mother, wearing a dark green silk suit, entered her room. "Is the bride almost ready? Your friends are gathering in the living room."

"Yes, I just have to fix these flowers in my hair," said Hazel. She'd chosen to wear a simple white lace, V-neck dress with capped sleeves. Simple but elegant to match her surroundings and this special event.

Her father knocked on the door and entered. "Is my daughter ready for me?"

Hazel and her mother turned as he walked over to them. "The two most beautiful women in the world," he murmured and kissed each of them on the cheek.

"I'll walk you, Helena, into the ceremony and come back for you, Hazel. Mike looks like he's more than ready for you to arrive. It's a good thing Jed is standing beside him to keep him calm."

After her parents left the room, Hazel glanced at her image in the mirror, once again surprised to see herself in a wedding dress with a precious baby bump. The love she shared with Mike had happened quickly, yet it felt as if it was part of a plan that was bigger than they could ever have imagined. A life destined to become shared with many.

Bringing her thoughts back to the present, Hazel smiled at her father and held out her arm for him to take.

Walking into the living room, she paused to gaze at her friends, old and new, waiting for her there. It seemed appropriate that Eugenie "GG" Wittner was among them because she was very much a matriarch of Lilac Lake.

Hazel lifted her eyes to Mike, and a silent message of love passed between them. She stepped forward to meet him and looked down at Jed, who stared up at her with a wonderous look while he stood proudly next to Mike.

Hazel prayed he'd always be part of their lives.

Mike's fingers covered hers, and she gazed at him, ready to face the future with him by her side.

# # # # #

Thank you for reading *Love's Match*. If you enjoyed this book, please help other readers discover it by leaving a review on Amazon, Goodreads, BookBub, or your favorite site. It's such a nice thing to do.

Sign up for my newsletter and get a free story. I keep my newsletters short and fun with giveaways, recipes, and the latest must-have news about me and my books. Welcome! Here's the link:

https://BookHip.com/RRGJKGN

About The Author

A *USA Today* Best-Selling Author, Judith Keim is a hybrid author who both has a publisher and self-publishes. Ms. Keim writes heart-warming novels about women who face unexpected challenges, meet them with strength, and find love and happiness along the way. Her best-selling books are based, in part, on many of the places she's lived or visited and on the interesting people she's met, creating believable characters and realistic settings her many loyal readers love. Ms. Keim loves to hear from her readers and appreciates their enthusiasm for her stories.

Ms. Keim enjoyed her childhood and young-adult years in Elmira, New York, and now makes her home in Boise, Idaho, with her husband and their lovable miniature Dachshunds, Wally and Kacy, and other members of her family.

While growing up, she was drawn to the idea of writing stories from a young age. Books were always present, being read, ready to go back to the library, or about to be discovered. All in her family shared information from the books in general conversation, giving them a wealth of knowledge and vivid imaginations.

"I hope you've enjoyed this book. If you have, please help other readers discover it by leaving a review on Amazon, Goodreads, Bookbub, or the site of your choice. And please check out my other books and series:"

The Hartwell Women Series

The Beach House Hotel Series

Fat Fridays Group

The Salty Key Inn Series

The Chandler Hill Inn Series

Seashell Cottage Books

The Desert Sage Inn Series

Soul Sisters at Cedar Mountain Lodge

The Sanderling Cove Inn Series

The Lilac Lake Inn Series

The Lilac Lake Books

"ALL THE BOOKS ARE NOW AVAILABLE IN AUDIO on Audible, iTunes, Findaway, Kobo and Google Play! So fun to have these characters come alive!"

Ms. Keim can be reached at **www.judithkeim.com**

And to like her author page on Facebook and keep up with the news, go to: **http://bit.ly/2pZWDgA**

To receive notices about new books, follow her on Book Bub: **https://www.bookbub.com/authors/judith-keim**

And here's a link to where you can sign up for her periodic newsletter! **http://bit.ly/2OQsb7s**

She is also on Twitter @judithkeim, LinkedIn, and Goodreads. Come say hello!

Acknowledgments

As always, I am eternally grateful to my team of editors, Peter Keim and Lynn Mapp, my book cover designer, Lou Harper, and my narrator for Audible and iTunes, Angela Dawe. They are the people who take what I've written and help turn it into the book I proudly present to you, my readers! I also wish to thank my coffee group of writers who listen and encourage me to keep on going. Thank you, Peggy Staggs, Lynn Mapp, Cate Cobb, Nikki Jean Triska, Joanne Pence, Melanie Olsen, and Megan Bryce. And to you, my fabulous readers, I thank you for your continued support and encouragement. Without you, this book would not exist. You are the wind beneath my wings.